An Adventure in ARIZONA

LAS MYSTERIES

BOOK 2

DONNA WREN CARSON

ARPress
45 Dan Road Suite 5
Canton MA 02021

Hotline: 1(800) 220-7660
Fax: 1(855) 752-6001

Ordering Information:
Quantity sales. Special discounts are available on quantity purchases by corporations, associations, and others. For details, contact the publisher at the address above.

Printed in the United States of America.

ISBN-13:   Paperback   979-8-89330-745-0

Library of Congress Control Number: 2024902826

Dedication

I dedicate this book to my incredible sister
Debra Armstrong Saltou and her son Aaron Ray Saltou.
If Debbie had not moved to Arizona, the concept would never
have entered into my imagination. Thank you both.

Summary

Leira and her new best friends Addy and Skye, are thrilled when Leira's Mom, Mrs. MacGregor, invites them to Arizona to visit her sister for winter school break. Skye has never flown on an airplane, and Addy has never stayed at a hotel. However, that is only the beginning of the adventure. In Arizona, the girls receive an invitation to spend three nights in the mountains camping with Leira's eighteen-year-old cousin Luke who is an eagle scout. The adventure brings them in contact with Indian lore, reptiles, animals, and much more. However, the trip turns into a nightmare when the group confronts mysterious happenings and a tragic accident find them in mortal danger!

Prologue

It was a bitter February morning in New England when I awoke to the shrill sound of my alarm. Hitting the button to shut it off, I scrunched down under my warm, toasty blankets. It was then that I heard the comforting sound of heat wafting upwards through the vents. Usually, I would grab my robe or a blanket and snuggle down in front of them while the heat radiated around me. However, today was different. Today, I was waiting anxiously for an answer about my upcoming winter vacation. The hardest part was being unable to say anything to my two best friends. My mom said if I spilled a word, then my friends and I would not be going anywhere!

Contents

Chapter 1

What Secret?

Skye, Addy, and I waited anxiously in the all-purpose room at J.P. Gooding Elementary School for my mom to pick us up. My new friends had known me since sixth grade had begun in the fall. While twirling a piece of her wavy, reddish-brown hair around her finger, Skye studied my expression, squinted her eyes, and asked, "Leira, why do you look so excited? What's going on?"

I responded cautiously, "Well, all I can say is that it has to do with our winter vacation. If I say anything else, then neither of you will have a chance to do something extremely exciting."

Addy stated irritably, "You can't just say something like that and not tell us what's happening! We're your best friends, and you know you can trust us."

Grimacing, I replied, "I know, but I don't want to let you down if it doesn't happen."

Luckily, (for me anyways), a student from Addy's class named Jeffrey approached and we abruptly stopped talking. Jeffrey was a nasty bully and, he had an enormous crush on Addy. The worst part though, was that a few weeks before, his family had moved next door to Addy's home.

He stopped in front of us gazing at Addy and said with a cocky drawl, "Addy, now that you and I are neighbors, I'll be able to walk you home when the weather's better. Your friends", he added, (with a sneer), "can tag along—if they want."

Skye gave Jeffrey a piercing look and stepped in front of Addy. Angrily, she exclaimed, "I've told you more than once to leave Addy alone! Leira, Addy and I walk together—just the THREE of us! Understand?"

Jeffrey taunted Skye by exclaiming, "Get out of my way freckle face, or you'll be sorry!"

I moved closer to Skye. We stood together in front of Addy and faced Jeffrey like a brick wall. With a barely concealed grin, Skye responded boldly, "If you get within twenty feet of us while walking to school, you'll have to deal with my older brother Liam." Smiling confidently, she added, "If you don't know him, then you'd better ask your snotty friends before it's too late!"

While Jeffrey looked shaken by Skye's statement, I added quickly, "And if you're not afraid of Liam, then I'm sure you've heard about that creepy recluse who lives at the old Grimly Manor in our neighborhood. You've probably heard about the stories of what happens to those who bother him OR his friends, and WE happen to be his friends!"

Jeffrey's face paled a bit. Glancing away, he said angrily, "Someday you'll be sorry you said that." Then looking straight at me he added, "I'll start by cutting off that long hair of yours Leira!"

Before I had a chance to respond, Jeffrey was gone. I nervously grabbed hold of my honey-brown hair, which was now six inches past my waist and began to twist it around my hands. Skye noticed, and said, "Don't worry Leira; he wouldn't dare do anything after what we just told him."

Addy chuckled softly and said, "Yeah Leira, you seriously got him good and scared by mentioning Mr. Grimly. Everyone is terrified of going anywhere near his house or the graveyard surrounding it. That was perfect! Did you see his eyes bug out when you told him Mr. Grimly was our friend?"

We covered our mouths, laughing uncontrollably and before I could say another word about my secret, I saw my mom walk in the room to bring us home. Immediately, I stopped laughing and whispered urgently, "Be quiet, here comes my mom. Do not say anything about a secret. I promise to tell you later." Apparently, 'the secret' had slipped their minds when Jeffrey approached us.

Addy looked around anxiously for her younger sister Josie, who she finally spotted sitting with her second grade friends. Addy called out, "Josie! Come on. We're leaving now." Josie hurried over to catch up, and we followed my mom to her car for the short drive home.

On the way home, Mom asked Skye and Addy, "Have either of your parents made plans for winter vacation? It's only a few weeks away."

Addy replied dismally, "I don't know. I guess I'll spend it with Skye and Josie. I know you and Leira are going to Arizona for vacation." Then she looked at me and whispered softly, "You're so lucky, Leira."

Skye added, "My parents are both working, so I guess I'm stuck home with my brother Liam."

My mother responded, "I have a little surprise for all of you." Skye, Addy and I looked at one another in anticipation. Mom continued, "I'm having a dinner party this weekend, and all of you are invited, including both your families and Mr. Grimly! Your parents and Mr. Grimly have accepted, so it should be a terrific time."

Skye leaned over to me and whispered sarcastically, "That's the awesome secret?"

Frustrated, I looked at her and said softly, "Shh, we'll talk about it later."

Addy, polite as always, replied, "That sounds neat, Mrs. MacGregor. What day is the party?"

Mom replied, "We're having it on Saturday, around four o'clock. Your mother is coming over early to help me get things ready, and Skye's mom is bringing two of her unique Irish recipes. By the way, Leira, you and Skye need to practice your step dancing because I'm planning to have you perform for everyone!" Skye and I grimaced at one another.

After pulling into our driveway, I asked, "Mom, could Skye and Addy do their homework over our house?"

She responded, "Not today Leira. We have to go grocery shopping before this ice storm hits. You'll have to do your homework when we get back."

I looked at Skye and Addy and in discouragement said, "I'm sorry, I'll call you later. If we can't get together this afternoon, at least tomorrow is Friday, so we'll be able to talk then."

Knowing that my mom was still listening, I didn't dare mention 'the secret'. I glanced back over my shoulder before going inside and watched my friends as they walked the last short distance to their homes. It was obvious they were disappointed that I hadn't told them the real secret.

Addy's house was next door to the left of mine. Before she went inside, I watched her brush back her dark-brown, almost black, bangs from her forehead.

Skye, whose house was directly across the street, was standing outside banging on the door. Apparently, her brother Liam was not answering.

After grocery shopping and finishing my homework, I called Skye's house and finally found out from her obnoxious brother that she and her parents had gone out to dinner. When I phoned Addy, her mother said she was still working on her homework.

I was actually relieved that neither of them could talk because I wanted to tell them together about the secret surprise. In addition, I absolutely did not want to take the chance that either of my parents would pick up the phone while I was talking.

School wasn't cancelled on Friday because the expected ice storm turned out to be mostly rain. Skye, Addy and I only talked together for a few minutes during the drive to school and back home. All I could whisper to them was, "Tomorrow's Saturday. We'll have lots of time to talk before the party."

Addy replied quietly, "My mom is going to your house early, so maybe you can tell me then."

I responded, "That wouldn't be fair to Skye, so let's just wait." Addy didn't complain, but she displayed a slight frown on her face that reminded me of her seven-year-old sister Josie.

That night, before bed, I asked my mother if the vacation plans had worked out. She replied teasingly, "You'll just have to wait until tomorrow to find out."

I looked at her in frustration and pleaded, "Can't you tell me anything?"

Sympathetically, she responded, "One of them is definitely going, but I'm not telling you who."

Anxiously, I asked, "What about the other one?"

Mom replied, "I've been promised an answer tomorrow." As she softly closed the door, she whispered, "Goodnight—Sweet dreams."

Chapter 2

An Invitation

On Saturday, Skye and Addy arrived after lunch. Immediately, they both demanded to know what the secret was. Glancing from one to the other, I finally replied reluctantly, "I can't tell you. WAIT! Before you both tackle me, I'll tell you this much—we'll all find out after dinner." Barraging me with questions, I shook my head desperately and replied, "No! My mom hasn't even told me everything."

Skye and Addy looked disappointed because they knew I wasn't lying.

Trying to cheer them up by changing the subject, I looked at Skye and said cheerfully, "My mom says your mother is bringing two of her homemade Irish recipes. Do you know what they are?"

Skye replied, "I know she's making my favorite soup—'Potato and leek'." Addy and I looked at her suspiciously, and then I asked, "What the heck are leeks?"

Skye responded, "They're something like an onion. Don't look so horrified! The soup is awesome, and once you smell it, I know you'll love it too." Addy and I looked a bit skeptical, but Addy said, "I'll definitely try some."

Skye continued, "I think she's also making my dad's favorite dinner. It's somewhat expensive, so she usually only makes it for his birthday. Actually, it's really yummy."

"Well?" I asked, "What is it?"

Skye replied, "It's called 'Pheasant a la Kerry gold'." Addy searched for something positive to say and finally remarked, "I'm sure it's probably very good."

Stifling a laugh, I looked over at Addy and said, "Someday, I'll tell you about the time my grandfather and uncle brought home a pheasant after hunting, but not today." Then, switching my tone of voice, I asked Addy, "Do you know what your mother is bringing?"

Addy tucked a piece of her blackish hair behind her ear as she responded enthusiastically, "Yes! My mom's bringing my favorite Welsh dishes. She's bringing Welsh Rarebit for an appetizer."

Skye gasped in horror. Then, she spit out, "You actually like eating rabbits? Yuck! That is disgusting! I'm not getting within ten feet of it!"

Addy started laughing and immediately said, "No, no, not rabbit but rarebit, 'R-A-R-E-B-I-T'. It's an awesome, thick cheese sauce, which you dip pieces of toasted, flavored bread into. It's delicious!"

Skye sighed in relief and said, "I thought you were crazy. So anyway, you said she was bringing your favorite dishes. What else is she bringing?"

Addy replied still smiling, "The other dish is called 'Ffest Y Cybydd'"

Bewildered, I asked, "Excuse me? What did you say?"

Addy laughed again and said, "That's Welsh for 'The Misers Feast'. Our whole family loves it." She continued in a dreamy voice, "It's a casserole filled with potatoes, onions and bacon, then cooked until it melts in your mouth." Her eyes rolled up, and I heard her stomach growl in reply to her thoughts.

Enthusiastically, I replied, "All right, I'll try some of that." Skye nodded in agreement.

Addy said excitedly, "Don't worry! I've saved the best for last. She's also bringing a dessert called 'Dinca Fala', which is like apple strudel, but ten times better. Leira, what's your mom making?"

I replied, "She's keeping it secret, but I'm hoping it's not what I think it is."

Skye asked suspiciously, "Why, what do you think it is?"

"Well…" I stammered out, "The most traditional Scottish dinner includes a main dish called 'haggis' and it's usually served with neeps and tatties."

Confused, Skye interrupted, "Could you repeat that in English?"

I answered, "Well, neeps are just turnips and tatties are potatoes."

Addy said encouragingly, "That doesn't sound too terrible, except I don't like turnips much. But, what is 'haggis'?"

Looking at her, I responded evasively, "It's made from a bunch of stuff, like meat, oatmeal, onions and other things. Then you stuff it into a casing, like hotdogs are, and then cook them. You'll have to taste it and see what you think. It's a popular dish!"

Skye questioned me suspiciously, "Then why did you say you hoped it wasn't what you thought it was?"

I replied, "Well, it's not my favorite thing to eat."

Addy asked pointedly, "What kind of meat is in this haggis?"

Directing my gaze to Addy, I replied, "You sure don't miss a thing! OK, here's the deal, it's made with lamb, sheep's liver and heart mixed with suet, which is some kind of fat and then stuffed into a casing made from sheep's stomach."

As Skye and Addy gasped in horror, Skye blurted out, "You're lucky you told me now because if I had tried that and then found out what it was, I would have never had spoken to you again! You've actually eaten it?"

Nodding my head, I replied, "I didn't have any choice because my mom made me. I might be Scottish, but that doesn't mean I like all Scottish food!"

Addy shook her head in despair and replied, "My parents are extremely strict on manners. We have to eat whatever we're served without complaining, so I hope your mom didn't make it."

I grimaced, and replied, "I'm sorry Addy. My parents usually make me try one little bite of something new, but they never make me eat anymore if I seriously don't like it—as long as I'm polite. I hope that she won't make it or if she does, you'll like it. Try and remember that a lot of people actually enjoy it!"

Addy's mom arrived in the early afternoon and within an hour, the house gradually filled with delicious aromas. About a half hour later, we glanced out my bedroom window and saw Skye's mom and dad walking over with a large covered platter and an enormous soup tureen. Shortly before four o'clock, the doorbell rang and we saw Addy's dad with her little sister Josie.

Excitedly, I said, "That's means we can go downstairs!" As we entered the dining room, we looked around in amazement. Our parents had decorated the room with Celtic imagery. It was beautiful! They had placed items from each of our Scottish, Welsh and Irish heritages everywhere. Mrs. Finnegan had brought an Irish lace tablecloth and linens. Mrs. Davies had hung a large tapestry that her grandmother had embroidered of the Welsh dragon. My mom had set out her Scottish thistle china, which was over a hundred years old. In every nook and cranny was something from our unique Celtic origins. In addition, playing softly in the background, were lilting Irish ballads.

The doorbell rang again and Mom asked, "Leira, could you please answer that? It's most likely Mr. Grimly and I think he has a surprise for you!"

As Skye, Addy and I raced to the door, I said, "We haven't seen Mr. Grimly in three weeks. I'm so happy he's coming tonight!"

I opened the door and much to my horror he was wearing one of his masks. I took his hand and led him in. I asked, "Why are you wearing that mask? You know we like you better without one." From underneath the mask, we heard a small chuckle.

Mr. Grimly replied, "Girls, you know I haven't seen you for a while, but there's a reason for that. Now don't be shocked when I take off the mask."

All three of us became uneasy at that remark. We knew how terribly scarred he had become since a fire had severely burned him when he was a child. But we had gotten used to his features; including what little remained of his nose, ears and lips. He was such a kind and generous man. As he slowly removed his mask, the three of us gasped in amazement. I stated excitedly, "Mr. Grimly, you have a nose!"

He replied happily, "Yes I do, thanks partly to your parents, Leira! They have been driving me over to the plastic surgeon to have reconstructive surgery and my nose was the first part. Do you like it?"

Hugging him, Skye replied, "It's fantastic!" Addy and I followed up with hugs, too.

Mom and Dad appeared and welcomed Mr. Grimly warmly. Mom said, "Everything's ready, so come on in!"

Just then, our puppies, Fluffums, Katie and Shuger, came bounding around the corner and jumped on Mr. Grimly. Obviously, they had picked up their mother's scent on him. All three of them licked away at his hands until he said, "All right there, girls! It's exciting to see you too, but I'll need to wash my hands again before dinner." As he walked toward the sink, he looked back at us and said, "My, how they've grown since I last saw them."

Mr. Grimlys' dog Puffin was the mother of the three pups, who were now almost four months old. For Christmas, Mr. Grimly had given one to Skye, Addy and me for helping him and Puffin. Whenever my friends came over, they usually brought their dogs with them, so the pups could play together.

The dinner was set out in the center of the kitchen island, buffet-style. Each item had a description card, so we knew what we were eating. My mother called everyone into the dining room and said, "Before we eat, Mrs. Finnegan would like us to stand holding hands while she gives a traditional Irish blessing on this gathering."

We bowed our heads in silence and listened to the beautiful blessing— at least it sounded beautiful in the Irish Gaelic language Skye's mother spoke. But, at the same time, I couldn't help but wonder if my mother had made 'haggis'.

After Mrs. Finnegan finished, Mom said, "All right, I'll turn the music back on while all of you take your plates into the kitchen. I hope you're all hungry!" Skye, Addy and I waited for everyone to go first because we thought our parents wouldn't be watching what we put on our plates. However, Addy's mom Aiselin was the last to get up, and she had Addy's younger sister Josie in tow. Her mom stopped next to Addy and whispered in her soft musical accent, "You know the rules. You need to try a little bit of everything."

Addy pleaded, "But Mom, what if there's something really horrible?"

Steely-eyed, she replied in the same soft tone, "Addy, one bite is not going to kill you. Now, do as I say or you're going to be terribly disappointed at the end of the meal."

Dismally, Addy nodded her head. As her mother went to the kitchen with Josie, Addy whispered to me, "Leira, I wish you'd never told me what haggis is made of."

I replied softly, "Sorry Addy, but maybe she didn't make it. Let's go see."

When Skye, Addy and I walked into the kitchen, the delicious aroma overwhelmed us. Our tummies grumbled loudly, and we suppressed our giggles of embarrassment. The first course was the soup and appetizers. We each took a small bowl of Mrs. Finnegan's potato and leek soup and some of Mrs. Davies Welsh rarebit. As we returned to the dining room, almost everyone else was finishing up and heading back to the kitchen. We sat down, and as Addy scoffed down her mom's cooking, Skye and I tentatively took a small bite. After my first taste of the rarebit, I looked up at Addy and exclaimed, "Wow! This is terrific! Let's skip everything else and eat just this!"

Our parents listened with interest as Skye said, "Try the soup, Leira."

Addy and I both took a spoonful, and after Addy tasted hers, she said to Skye, "You're right Skye. This is the best soup I've ever had!"

I nodded in agreement, as I downed another mouthful. Glancing up, I saw Skye's mother grinning proudly. Addy's mother, who was also watching, said, "Addy, leave some room for the main courses and dessert."

Josie whined, "I hate both of them!" But, Mrs. Davies made sure she tried each one to her satisfaction.

After everyone had gone back to the kitchen, we finished up. Then, reluctantly, we grasped our plates and headed off for the dreaded 'main course'. When we got to the buffet, Addy's mom was still there with Josie. She gave Addy a piercing look. Addy nodded, understanding that she had to try everything that she had never tried before.

Addy encouraged us, saying, "Try the 'Miser's Feast'." Skye and I scooped up a small portion, and then looked at what was next. Skye's mom made the 'Pheasant a la Kerry gold'. It looked like thick sliced chicken, with a small helping of vegetables surrounding each portion, and covered in sauce. We each took a piece while Skye encouraged, "Don't worry, it's really pretty good."

Next, came the dreaded haggis. Addy looked at the thinly sliced portions before stabbing the smallest one, and placed it on her plate. Quickly, I slid one onto my plate also.

Addy turned to me asking, "Why are you having some?"

I replied, "I said it wasn't my favorite food, but if you have to eat some then I'll have some too."

Addy said, "Thanks Leira. I honestly appreciate that." We both looked at Skye expectantly. Staring back at us, she sarcastically asked, "What? Are you crazy? I'm sorry, but I'm not touching that!" Addy and I were disappointed. Skye was usually the bravest one amongst us, but apparently, that didn't include food.

When we returned to the dining room, my parents and Addy's gave us looks of approval. But, when Skye's mother, Fiona, saw her plate, she said, "Skye, you haven't got any haggis on your plate. It's a particularly remarkable Scottish dish and Mrs. MacGregor spent a lot of time preparing it." Standing up, Mrs. Finnegan reached out her hand and said, "Give me your plate and I'll get some for you."

After her mother left, Skye looked at Addy and I in horror. She whispered to us, "I can't believe she's doing this! I bet if my brother Liam had been here, she wouldn't have said a word."

I asked, "Why isn't Liam here?"

Skye replied quietly, "He's at a birthday party and sleepover. 'Lucky for him'!"

Skye's mom returned with a plate full of two portions of haggis, and the pheasant was gone.

Skye mumbled, "Mom, you know I like your pheasant, so why do I have to eat two slices of haggis?"

Her mom looked at her without a bit of sympathy and responded, "Because, I knew you would want to make your hostess happy!" Then, she smiled.

The three of us looked dismally at our plates and began eating. I started with what I thought was the worst, 'the pheasant'. Skye watched me while I tried it. After finishing my first bite, I told Addy, "It really tastes yummy, especially with the sauce. It doesn't taste anything like the horrible pheasant Grandpa and Uncle Chuck cooked."

Addy tried hers and replied, "You're right Leira, it's good!" Skye smiled happily.

Next, we tasted the 'Miser's Feast'. Addy gave a nod of encouragement, then Skye and I ate a spoonful. Addy could tell from our expressions that we liked it. She smiled contently.

Next, came the dreaded haggis. I whispered, "It's not that bad." As my mom watched me, I took a bite, chewed quickly and swallowed. I said to Skye and Addy, "Really, it's alright!"

At that moment, Fluffums, Katie and Shuger came racing into the room. My mom exclaimed, "I thought you girls had put them outside! Leira, get those pups out of here now."

I jumped up, yelling over my shoulder, "Mom, I'm sorry. I thought they were outside!"

During the commotion, Skye grabbed one piece of haggis and threw it unnoticed under the table. My dog Fluffums, headed for me from the far side of the room and scoffed it down on her way! Quickly Skye threw the second chunk under the table, and Shuger grabbed that tidbit. Unaware of what Skye was doing, Addy took a small piece of haggis and started chewing. At first, her mouth contorted in disgust, but a few seconds later, her face relaxed and she finished her piece. Skye looked at her in total astonishment.

When I returned from letting the puppies outside, I looked at Skye and Addy and whispered, "What's going on? Did something happen?"

Skye gazed at me and said, "Addy just ate all of her haggis. She's one tough cookie!"

I quickly turned to Addy and asked, "Are you all right?"

She responded, "Yeah, I actually kind of liked it."

Skye and I looked at each other in disbelief, and I said, "Well, you learn something new every day! Then I noticed Skye's dish was empty, so I asked, "You liked it too?"

Skye responded, "Oh, absolutely! The tummy it's sitting in is extremely happy."

I heard Mr. Grimly trying unsuccessfully to contain his laughter and looked him directly in the eyes. He was still trying cover up his reaction and suddenly I knew Skye had done something she was trying to hide.

I said skeptically to her, "Somehow, I don't believe that."

Addy looked at me and replied, "I don't either."

I was sure I would find out eventually just what had happened. For dessert, we had Mrs. Davies 'Dinca Fala' (Welsh apple strudel) and, to my surprise, my mom made my favorite, 'Scottish shortbread'.

After dessert, my mom cleared her throat and said, "I have a fantastic announcement." Skye, Addy and I looked up in anticipation.

Mom proceeded, "As you know, Leira and I are going to Arizona for winter vacation." Then, pointedly she looked at Skye, Addy and me, and announced with a knowing grin, "Addy, Skye, you'll be pleased to know that your parents have given their permission for you to go with us."

The three of us looked at each other in total shock, and then began jumping up and down, squealing in delight! I couldn't believe it! Even though my mom had told me one of them was coming, I was ecstatic to learn that both of them were! I could never imagine what an adventure we would stumble into.

Chapter 3

The Flight and Hotel

The day before the flight, the three of us went over our packing lists for the fifth time. We were each allowed one large suitcase (to check into baggage), and one carry-on backpack that would contain drawing supplies, a book, CD player and any other small entertaining things we could squeeze into it. I said to Skye and Addy, "Well, I think we've got everything!" Then, with a huge grin, I asked, "Can you believe we're going from ten degrees outside snowing, to eighty degrees and sunny?"

Skye replied, "That sounds awesome..., but there's one thing that makes me nervous."

I almost choked while asking, "Why are YOU nervous? You're not afraid of anything. Anyway, you're leaving your worst nightmare behind— your brother Liam."

Skye replied, slightly embarrassed, "Well, I've never flown before and I've definitely never been two thousand miles from home."

Hoping to calm her nerves, I said enthusiastically, "Skye, flying isn't only safe— it's really fun!"

Addy nodded in encouragement and added, "You'll love it! I've only been on one plane, and that was when we moved here from Wisconsin last year. The flight attendants were extremely polite. They gave me a pillow; a blanket and an airline pin to wear near the end of the flight for being such a good flyer!"

Skye asked, "How long was your flight?"

Addy considered and replied, "I think about four hours, but I'm not really sure because I fell asleep for a while."

Skye said thoughtfully, "The airplane makes me nervous, but I trust you guys. I just hope it's as fun as you make it sound. Is it alright if I sit in the aisle seat because I really don't want to look out the window?"

Happily, I responded, "I've got no problem with that because I usually fight for the window seat!"

Addy groaned, "Hey! I wanted the window seat too."

I replied, "All right, here's the deal, we're going to change planes in Dallas—that's in Texas, so you can have the window seat from here to there and I'll take it from Dallas to Arizona. Alright?"

Addy said, "That's sounds okay, but do you know what I'm really excited about, besides Arizona?"

Skye and I responded simultaneously, "No, what?"

Addy replied excitedly, "I've never stayed at a really nice hotel before, so that's going to be super special!"

Suppressing a chuckle, I said, "Well, I'll tell you one really cool thing about where we're staying."

Addy and Skye both questioned, "What?"

Excitedly, I answered, "Our room is a suite (two rooms) and it has a Jacuzzi in it!"

Skye and Addy looked at one another in delight. As Addy was about to say something, my mom yelled, "Skye, Addy! It's time you went home because we're leaving at six o'clock tomorrow morning."

Excitedly, I said goodnight, but I don't think any of us got much sleep that night. Fluffums sensed my excitement and wouldn't leave my side. One part of the trip that made me sad was leaving her behind. I hoped Dad, my other dog Lucky, and my cat Emmy would keep Fluffums happy until I returned.

The following morning, Dad piled our luggage into the trunk, picked up Addy and Skye, and then we headed off to the airport.

At the airport, Skye, Addy and I followed my mom to the curbside check-in where we dropped off our bags and got our boarding tickets. With only our backpacks slung over our shoulders, we proceeded towards our terminal. As we approached, Skye was about to experience her first encounter with security. Calmly, my mother told us to take off our jackets and place them, our purses, and backpacks on the conveyor belt to be scanned. Skye gazed uncomfortably at the conveyor. Then, after quickly studying the security scanner she had to walk through, she whispered to me with a hint of panic in her eyes, "Leira, what happens when I walk through that thing?"

Smiling in sympathy, I replied, "Don't worry, Addy and I will go first and show you." Skye nodded in relief. Actually, my mom went first, and the security officer told her to remove her sneakers and place them on the conveyor. After she finished, I smelled a stinky odor and whispered to her, "Mom, I think you should get some new sneakers." She didn't look happy at my comment.

Mom, Addy and I walked through security without a hitch, but when Skye walked through, the beeper went off, scaring her half to death.

Skye burst out in panic, "What did I do?" The attendant calmed her by saying, "I'm sure everything is OK. Just step over here."

My mother was standing a few feet from Skye and spoke quietly to her, saying it was probably just some jewelry or something. The security attendant ran a wand scanner over Skye and found a few spots of concern. It turned out that her watch, earrings and ankle bracelet were the culprits! After they let us pass, mom put her stinky sneakers back on, and we headed toward our gate (B-20). As we neared it, Addy and I noticed a stand selling 'Critter Pillows'. They were stuffed animals shaped to wrap around your neck during a flight to help you sleep. I pleaded with my mom, but she adamantly exclaimed, "NO WAY!"

We had an hour left until our flight. The three of us were reading when Mom went off to the ladies room. She was gone for some time, and when I looked for her, my eyes briefly fastened on the 'Critter Pillow' stand. I noticed a woman buying several pillows. I thought to myself, "Well, some people are lucky."

A few moments later, a strange shadow hung over the pages of my book. I looked up and there in front of us, was my mom, holding FOUR

'Critter pillows'! She cheerfully asked, "Girls, which one do you want?" Happily, we chose the ones we wanted, and left the last one for her.

An announcement came over the loudspeaker stating they would begin boarding in fifteen minutes. The person also stated that there were several first-class seats still available and that if anyone would like to upgrade from coach to first class the cost would be twenty-five dollars. I noticed my mom thinking about something, and before I could figure out what, she looked at me with a pinch of excitement and asked, "Well, do you want to go for it? Do you think they'll have four seats?"

Ecstatically, I responded, "Yes! Please? Can we?"

Mom replied, "OK, let's go try." Skye and Addy followed us to the terminal desk. Mom spoke to the agent saying, "We'd like to upgrade to first class if possible. It was apparent by the look on my mom's face that four seats were unlikely, but the attendant responded, "Yes, we do." Mom glanced at me with a large grin and continued with the upgrade process. Nervously, Skye tugged at my sleeve and asked, "Leira what does 'First Class' mean? Will we have to do homework?"

Addy raised her eyebrows in disbelief while I explained to Skye, trying desperately not to laugh that we were not going into a classroom.

I responded, "Skye, 'first class' means you get the best seats on the airplane, and they're bigger and better seats. They even give you your food and drinks free, AND you get 'real' silverware! You're treated extra special."

Addy nodded and said, "I've heard about it, but obviously, I've never done it. I'll have to tell my parents how great it is before we take another trip."

I added, "Me neither, so this will be different for all of us. This is so cool!" Shortly afterwards, we boarded the plane for the first flight to Texas. After finding our seats, we noticed there were only two seats on each side because they were much wider than the 'coach' seats that we would have had. Addy took the window seat, with Skye next to her. I let my mom take the window seat on the other side because otherwise I wouldn't be able to talk to my friends. As the plane was taking off, I noticed Skye had a death grip on the arms of her seat. I reached over and gave her hand a quick squeeze while saying, "Don't worry; this is one of the fun parts." She glanced over at me and nodded with a tiny smile.

Excitedly, we realized the first class section of our airplane had a TV screen on the back of every seat. There was a huge selection of movies to choose from, and we each ended up watching different ones. Fully entertained and pausing only for breakfast, the flight literally 'flew' by. We landed in Dallas on time and disembarked from the plane.

We didn't have any trouble finding our next gate for our flight to Phoenix. Although disappointed we couldn't upgrade our seats on the second flight, we were thrilled when we boarded, and saw that this airplane also had TV's at every seat.

I told Skye and Addy as we took off, "There's a two hour time difference between Connecticut and Arizona, and even though we'll be arriving in Phoenix at one in the afternoon, it'll actually be three o'clock to us."

Addy inquired, "Who's picking us up? Is your cousin Brianna going to be there?"

I replied, "I doubt it because there probably won't be enough room for all of us."

The plane landed fifteen minutes early. We struggled through the crowd to get to the baggage claim area. Watching carefully for our bags, I said excitedly, "There's mine!"

Startled, by a shriek, I turned around anxiously to see what was going on. However, it turned out to be my Aunt Debbie, who had just given my mom a fright by tapping her on the shoulder. After gathering our bags, Aunt Debbie hurried us to the curb where Uncle Ray was waiting in his van.

We bustled into it while Uncle Ray stowed the luggage in the trunk, then set off towards Mesa where my Aunt and Uncle lived. The scenery fascinated Skye and Addy.

Addy exclaimed to me, "Wow! Look at all the cactus with flowers growing on them—and those mountains over there are almost glowing dark orange. I never imagined the desert would look anything like this!"

Pointing, I responded, "Actually we're heading towards those mountains. They're called the Superstition Mountains."

Intrigued, Skye asked, "What's the superstition?"

Aunt Debbie replied, "You'll get your answer to that tomorrow when we take you to the Ghost Mining Town."

I said, "Fantastic! I can't wait to show you everything there!"

Mom replied, "Let's just get settled into the hotel for now. Then we can rest for a few hours before Uncle Ray picks us up to get our car rental. After that we'll head over to Aunt Debbie's for dinner."

Skye asked hesitantly, "You're not going to make Haggis, are you, Mrs. Saltou?"

Aunt Debbie replied laughing, "No Skye, I'm not making Haggis, mostly because my family wouldn't eat it and neither will I."

Skye breathed a sigh of relief, and then inquired, "How much further is it to the hotel?"

I pointed out the window at an illuminated, light coral, unique property and stated, "We're here!"

Addy and Skye were both bug-eyed and responded in unison, "Wow!"

Mom checked us in, and then we took the elevator up to the seventh floor.

Skye, Addy and I bickered over who would open the door with the sliding key card. Mom took it from us and said, "We'll take turns." She slid the key through the lock, and when the green light blinked, she opened the door. After turning on the lights, Addy and Skye walked slowly into the room in utter amazement. As Skye headed around the corner into the next room, Addy stopped short at the double-sink counter, just to the left of the entrance hall. All around it were amenities, including soap, lotion, cotton balls, toothpaste, plastic cups, bottled water and much more. To the left of the sinks was a coffee maker and a pretty box filled with sugar, cream, tea, hot chocolate and two types of coffee. She slowly spun around and asked my mom in a hushed tone, "Mrs. MacGregor, are we allowed to use any of these things?"

Mom and I looked at each other, and tried extremely hard not to burst out in laughter. Mom replied smiling, "Addy, everything here is for us."

Addy responded in awe, "My dad loves these packets of coffee and sugar." Hesitantly she asked, "Do you think I could take a few home for him when we leave?"

Mom chuckled slightly and replied, "You can take as many as you like."

Just then, from an area around the corner to the left, I heard Skye squeal, "Hey, they left us homemade chocolate chip cookies on the beds!" Addy and I sprinted around the corner to see the adjoining bedroom. It had two queen-sized beds, a large TV with pay-per-view movies and a DVD player. I immediately jumped on the bed I wanted then shouted, "This one's mine!" My mother casually reminded me it was 'ours'. Skye and Addy jumped onto the other one. It was then that my friends gazed at the dimly lit section across from us and spotted the enormous sunk-in Jacuzzi nestled in the corner of the large living room! The three of us definitely would fit into it. Jumping off the beds, we ran into the adjoining room. I switched on the 'dimmer' lights and showed them how the Jacuzzi worked. There were mirrors surrounding it, with the lights twinkling above it. The rest of the room had a small dining/living room area with another over-sized TV.

Mom was busy unpacking and suggested we do the same. Then she lay down on the bed and read for a few minutes. She turned off the light in the bedroom and prior to shutting the adjoining door, said, "Don't leave the room, and please try and be quiet. Wake me up at five-thirty."

Chapter 4

Ghost Mining Town

After waking Mom, we hurried downstairs to wait for Uncle Ray. Soon thereafter, he pulled up, and to my surprise, my nineteen-year-old cousin Brianna was with him! After piling into the vehicle and leaving for the rental agency, I introduced Skye and Addy to Brianna. I was ecstatic to see her. Brianna exclaimed, "Oh Leira, your hair is below your waist!"

I replied, "Your hair looks darker and shinier than the last time I saw you." She blushed and thanked me as we chatted about everything that had taken place over the last year. I couldn't believe that she had graduated from high school and even had a part-time job before starting college in the fall.

We arrived at the car rental agency, and after my mom left the car to pick up our vehicle, I asked Uncle Ray, "Do you know what we're doing tomorrow?"

He responded, "Yes I do, and if you'd been paying attention earlier you would too." Grinning and letting out one of his sly, drawn-out chuckles, he continued, "I'm sure of one thing though, it'll be a long boring day for you."

I glanced at Skye and Addy, then whispered, "Don't worry, he's always joking around with everyone." Mom came back quickly and said, "Ok, I'm all set. Who wants to ride with me while I follow Uncle Ray home?" I looked expectantly at Brianna because I wanted to stay with her.

Thoughtfully, Brianna asked my mom, "Aunt Cate, do you have enough room in your car for all of us?"

Mom replied comically, "Well yes, except for Uncle Ray—who needs to drive his own vehicle home."

All of us shouted that we wanted to drive in Mom's rental car. Uncle Ray responded in a wounded voice, rubbing his eyes, "That's OK; I know you don't want to visit with me."

Mom said, "Ray, you could really use acting lessons." All of us clambered into Mom's awesome minivan. The ride to Aunt Debbie's was quick. Even before we were able to get completely out of the van, my twenty-year old cousin Tara bombarded us with bone-crunching hugs! She was so excited that we had finally arrived. I introduced her to my friends and after grabbing one of our bags; she led us to the front door of their large home. I gazed at the outside of the house as I slowly walked forward. The heavy suitcase I was carrying with both hands, bumped painfully against my knees, but with each step I took, I felt overwhelmed again by their homes' unique design. The light beige-pink stucco was so pretty. Since last year, they had planted cacti along the stone pathway leading to the doorway. As we entered, Addy gasped, "It's so awesome!"

The vaulted stairway across from the front door led up to the second floor. I smiled when I saw that Aunt Debbie had decorated the previously barren wall with several family portraits. A Queen Anne cherry wood grandfather clock by the base of the stairway captivated Skye, and as she glanced to the right, she noticed a matching piano in the living room. She looked back at me and stated, "Wow! I thought OUR new house was really cool."

Addy nodded her head in agreement.

I said to my friends, "The first time I saw Aunt Debbie's house was before it was finished. Even though it might seem quite large now, when everyone gets together, it's not quite big enough."

Skye asked, "Who's everyone?"

Addy, Skye and I followed Tara and Brianna into the living room and plunked down on the sofa as I considered Skye's question, then responded, "Well, besides Tara, Brianna and their brother Luke who lives here, there's also their two sisters Carrie and Becca. They only live a few miles away. Carrie has a two-year-old daughter named Hannah and Becca and her husband Tyler live in the same neighborhood with their daughter Lea, who's only four. Then, there's my oldest cousin Jenna, but she lives in Utah, so unfortunately you won't get to meet her— this time—anyway."

At that moment, Addy whispered into my ear, "Where's your cousin Luke?"

I asked Tara and Brianna, "Where's Luke hiding?"

Tara said, "I don't know." Then she proceeded to yell out, "Hey Mom! Where is Luke? Leira and her friends want to meet him."

Aunt Debbie replied, "He's in the computer room working on something special for the three of you. But I can't tell you now—I'm getting ready to make dinner."

Intrigued, I quickly asked, "What's he working on and what are we doing tomorrow?" I noticed Skye and Addy were listening intently.

Aunt Debbie and Mom gave a quick sneaky look at one-another. Then Mom replied, "Well, to answer your second question for the second time, tomorrow we are going up to the Gold Mining Ghost Town."

I felt stupid that I had forgotten that she had already told us. I guess I was so tired and excited from the trip that I didn't remember. Apparently, Skye and Addy did not forget, so they prodded me again to tell them more about it, but I refused to tell them anything.

For dinner, that night, my mom and Aunt Debbie made my grandmother's famous spaghetti and meatballs recipe, salad, and fresh-made buttery, garlic bread. My cousin Luke finally appeared as Aunt Debbie put food on the table. He was a quiet, good-natured, eighteen-year old Eagle Scout who had accomplished a lot throughout his training. He was rather tall with short, dark hair and a few freckles lay scattered over his nose and cheeks. I had gotten to know Luke over several years and I kind of thought of him like my 'big brother'.

While everyone was eating, I quizzed Luke on the 'special treat' he had planned for us. Seeming perplexed, he asked, "What are you talking about? All I know is that you're going to the Ghost Mining Town tomorrow."

He had the same mischievous look on his face as Uncle Ray did when he was kidding us, so I replied casually, "Well, I guess you'll just hang out with your friends and disappear as usual." He looked directly at me with a smile I had never seen before.

We drove back to the hotel after dinner, even though it was only eight o'clock. For us, it was ten o'clock at night because of the time change. As I crawled into bed, I asked my mom, "Do you know what Luke is up to?"

Mom replied with a huge yawn, "I know a little, but it'll be best if you find out tomorrow evening when we're at Aunt Debbie's."

I gave my mom a shove and said, "Thanks a lot."

She replied wearily, "You're welcome. Night-night."

The following morning I awoke early. I nudged my mom, but after a short groan, she was snoring again. I gave her another shove, and after seeing her eyes flutter, I decided to wake up my friends. Skye was closest in the bed next to me, so I crawled out of bed, gave her a poke, and asked in a hushed voice, "Skye, are you sleeping?" After a moment, she groggily replied, "Not anymore."

I replied, "I'm sorry for waking you up, but I can't wait to begin the day."

Rubbing her sleep-crusted eyes, she asked, "What time is it?"

I answered, "Seven o'clock, but for us that's nine o'clock." Then, I tentatively asked, "Would you help me wake up Addy?"

Skye replied sarcastically, "Yeah, right! I know how grumpy she is in the morning, but I'll help you if you get your mom up." I nodded in agreement, silently thinking that my mom was already half-awake.

Skye and I shook our intended victims (not too gently). Alarmed, my mom stammered out "What is it? Is everyone OK?"

While assuring my mom that everything was fine, I turned toward Addy as she yelled out, "What is it? I'm trying to sleep!" Skye responded by pushing her right off the bed! A loud thump reached our ears as she hit the floor.

Addy spouted out angrily, "Ouch! What did you do that for?"

Skye answered truthfully, "It was the best way to wake you up."

While Addy rubbed her sore hip and elbow, my mother asked concerned, "Are you alright Addy?"

Addy replied, "I guess so, but tomorrow morning, I'd just like to sleep in."

My mom replied, "We need to get up now."

Everyone slid out of bed except Addy, who raised herself off the carpet to get ready for the day's adventure. As the minutes ticked by, I could sense by my friend's questions that they were enthusiastic about exploring Arizona. By the time we went down to breakfast, they were uncontrollably excited. Mom and I couldn't answer questions fast enough.

After eating, my mom phoned Aunt Debbie to let her know we were on our way to her house. After arriving, I was thrilled to find out that Brianna was going with us. I asked Aunt Debbie, "What about Tara and Luke? Aren't they coming too?" Aunt Debbie replied, "Tara is working and Luke has something important he needs to take care of."

Uncle Ray had already gone to work, so Addy, Skye, Brianna, Aunt Debbie, Mom and I set off for our trip. It only took about thirty minutes to reach our destination. We were awestruck by the picturesque scenery along the way. We kept firing questions at Aunt Debbie about everything we saw. She answered everything she was able to, but finally said, "Just wait until Luke's with you, he'll be able to answer all of your questions."

We turned onto the dirt road at 'The Gold Mining Ghost Town', and I saw the excitement on Skye and Addy's faces. The realistic 'old west' look of the town captivated them. Brianna and I glanced at each other and smiled because we remembered the spooky, startling and funny moments we had shared from previous visits. We parked as far away as possible from the 'Bee Tree', which was a whopping, creepy looking tree inhabited by thousands of bees.

First, my mom took us on a historical open car train ride around the town. The conductor—Joshua was our guide for the one-and-a-half mile journey. He stopped the train every few minutes to explain the town's history. He told us there had been a gold strike in 1892, and that at the height of the gold rush, 4,000 people camped in and around the town.

Skye interrupted and asked, "What's the difference between a 'gold rush' and a 'gold strike'?"

He explained that a strike was when one or more miners found a large vein of gold, and a rush was when everyone else found out about it! Then, he tipped his hat and winked at Skye and said, "Thankee little lady! I just love it when a purty gal asks me a question that I know."

Skye's blush was noticeable even in the hot, bright sunlight. Then Joshua turned towards the landscape and told us about the hardships of the miners. He spooked us with the legend of the 'Lost Dutchman Mine'. A treasure was hidden somewhere in a mine beneath the beautiful but eerie Superstition Mountains that partially encircled us. The mine had become legendary.

He explained about the different types of plants and wildlife of the Sonoran Desert surrounding us; pointing to those within sight. Then his voice turned slightly ominous as he continued, "These Mountains were, and still are, sacred to the Native American Indians of this region. Many people who have traveled into the mountains in search of the treasure have disappeared, or been found dead. The ancestors of those Native American's have declared that those old prospector's spirits still roam the range. Even today, those who still search for the 'Lost Dutchman Mine' take many precautions to prepare for whatever may occur." Still, as I gazed at the Superstition Mountains, I found them hauntingly beautiful.

After getting off the train, we headed for the Gold Mining Tour. Mom and Aunt Debbie were claustrophobic (meaning they were afraid of small, dark, closed-in places) and refused to go, but Brianna, Addy, Skye and I bravely got in line. As we paid, the man handed each of us a small wooden club. My mother asked the attendant (who looked and sounded like he was actually a prospector from the 'old west'), "What are these for?"

He replied slowly, "Well, you know, sometimes we get bats down in the mines. So, these here are for y'all to swing at them, just in case."

Addy questioned nervously, "Are you serious?"

He raised a brow while rubbing his thick moustache and drawled, "Well, it hasn't happened in a while, so I think you'll be just fine. Now go on there, pretty gal and let Clarissa take ya on the tour."

The four of us glimpsed at one another suspiciously but got into line with the other five or so visitors. I took one last look over my shoulder towards my mom before entering the mine. She looked more nervous than I did.

We carefully walked down about twenty dusty old wooden stairs to a boarded-up wall, which turned out to be a creepy old elevator shaft.

Clarissa grabbed some type of knob or latch, and the wooden 'wall' laboriously opened making a loud scraping noise. She said, "Watch your step as you enter the elevator." We were alarmed when Clarissa told us to keep our 'bats' handy because about a week ago someone had actually whacked at one.

She explained that we were going to descend deep into the mine. Once the elevator started, I think it only took a few minutes, but it seemed much longer. When Clarissa opened the door at the bottom, a musty smell overtook us. As we walked along the cool, damp, barely lit passageway, she talked about the tools displayed on the walls, as well as the mining process.

Soon we came upon one small-unlit candle. Clarissa said, "If you're afraid of the dark, you might want to close your eyes."

Addy, slightly frightened, whispered to me, Skye and Brianna, "I wonder what she's going to do. Are you nervous too?" Before we could answer, everything went pitch black. Addy gasped and whispered, "I can't see anything."

Skye reassured her, saying, "It's alright Addy, grab hold of my hand."

Addy replied nervously, "I thought I was."

I said, "No Addy—that's my hand you're holding."

Skye asked nervously, "Well then, whose hand am I holding?"

Brianna whispered, "Don't worry, it's mine."

Clarissa stated, "This is all the miners had for light."

Before we uttered another word, the candle lit up, relieving our fears. Clarissa explained, "This candle is made of animal fat. Each miner only received four of them, and they all burned out fairly quickly."

At once, the reality of what the miners endured became real. As we followed our guide down the tunnel, we came to another door. Clarissa opened it and turned on few dim lights. As we entered a cavern-like area, I jumped in fright when I saw a decrepit miner—only to realize it was stuffed dummy! Then Addy screeched; "There's a rat on it!"

Brianna consoled her, "It's fake, just like the miner dude." She gave her a hug of reassurance.

Just as Addy breathed a sigh of relief, her heart froze as a bat came swooping towards her. Brianna hadn't seen it, but Skye and I did! The three of us screamed and raced towards Clarissa. A large man who had brought his family struck at it with his 'bat'. He didn't actually hit it, but it turned around and flew back towards the darkened tunnel.

Clarissa looked at us and said apologetically, "Sorry about that." The faint light of the exit became barely visible. I nudged Skye, pointing toward it while Clarissa finished the story of the trapped miner who survived nearly a month before rescue arrived. On the way out, we saw a sign saying we should tip the guide or give them a kiss! We did neither.

With our hearts still pounding, we thankfully saw my mom and Aunt Debbie. I didn't tell them that most of us had been frightened to death. After stopping to buy gifts and ice cream, we approached the next shop, which was an antique photography studio where you could dress up in 19th century clothes and have your picture taken. Mom asked, "Do you girls want to do this?"

Skye, Addy and I responded quickly, "YES!" Brianna was uncertain, but I convinced her to be in the picture. Upon entering the shop, we were amazed at the hundreds of outfits available.

Sherry, the woman who ran the place, asked each of us how we would like to dress. Addy responded, "A cowgirl." Sherry fitted Addy with heavy leather chaps, an old, worn-out, long-sleeve shirt, a vest, a hat, a holster and a rifle. She looked impressive.

Sherry then turned to me, and I replied, "A western lady." She gave me a beautiful, long gown, a large, wide hat with flowers, and a parasol.

Next was Skye's turn. She looked a bit doubtful, but said, "I'd like to be a gun-slinging sheriff." Sherry dressed her in western pants, a white shirt, and string tie, a holster with a gun, and a long, black ranger coat and hat. She completed her outfit with a fake mustache and two pistols.

Finally, it was Brianna's turn. We encouraged her to dress as a saloon girl. She wasn't hugely enthusiastic about it, but Mom asserted that it would make the picture perfect. Brianna looked uncomfortable in a deep-cut frilly dress, but stood bravely as Sherry painted her face with heavy makeup. Finally, she positioned us and took several photos. After removing our fancy clothing, she showed us five different pictures on the computer. Together, we decided which one was best. Then we headed off to an outdoor restaurant for lunch while she finished editing and printing our photos.

After lunch, we went back to the photography shop and picked up our pictures. They came out fantastic! We were all glad we took the time to have it done.

Excitedly, I asked Mom, "Can we go to the reptile museum next?"

She replied, "I'm really sorry Leira, but we're running out of time. Aunt Debbie needs to go home to baby-sit for Hannah."

I stated, "You're probably just saying that because you were so frightened by the tarantula last time!"

Aunt Debbie said, "No, Leira, it's not that. I do have to be home by three o'clock"

I knew Aunt Debbie watched my Cousin Carrie's two-year old daughter, so I replied, "Ok. But, can we at least go gold panning before we leave?"

Mom responded, "Of course! That's why we have just enough time— unless you'd rather look at reptiles?"

Skye, Addy and I looked at each other and agreed quickly that we'd rather pan for gold. When we reached the shack, the woman showed us how to pan for gold. Then, she briefly explained the difference between 'real gold' and 'fool's gold'. Each of us filled a tiny vial with a few bits of real gold, along with other shiny, colorful pieces. Some were beautiful, like the red garnet. As soon as we finished, we had to leave, but I was happy because I knew Skye, Addy and Brianna all had a terrific time.

Chapter 5

Ready to Camp

Upon arriving back at Aunt Debbie's house, my cousin Carrie raced out to meet us. She gave me an enormous hug and said, "I've missed you so much! When are your parents going to move here so we can see each other all the time?"

I replied, "Well, I don't think that's going to happen, but I'll keep my fingers crossed. Where's Hannah?" Carrie glanced towards the family room and whispered, "She's probably hiding. Here, take her little bear and see if you can persuade her to come out."

After introducing my friends to Carrie, we began to track down the little minx. We found her behind the sofa, and in no time, she was giggling uncontrollably. Meanwhile, Carrie left for work after saying; she'd be back for dinner. Addy, Skye and I spent the next few hours playing with Hannah. It was very warm outside, and the sun felt incredible. While Hannah took a nap, Tara and Brianna spent a few hours playing badminton with us.

Eventually, Addy, Skye and I became extremely hungry, so I ran in and asked Mom when and what we were going to have for dinner. Mom answered, "Well since you love Haggis so much, we've decided to give it a go."

Horrified, I replied, "No way. You're joking—aren't you?"

Aunt Debbie smiled and said, "Yes, she's joking, we're having tacos and—" Addy interrupted, "Awesome. That's my favorite."

I gave Addy a sour look, and then peered up at my mom. She knew I didn't like tacos. She replied chuckling, "We're also having chicken nuggets, french fries and tomato soup." A smile instantly appeared on my face.

At seven o'clock, everyone gathered for dinner. The only thing that Skye, Addy and I were actually thinking about was Luke's special adventure. Even though it was killing us, the three of us decided not to ask any questions because we knew that Uncle Ray and Luke would torture us with added suspense.

Finally, after eating homemade chocolate mayonnaise cake for dessert, Luke cleared his throat, and then asked Addy, Skye and me, "Would the three of you like to go camping in the canyons and mountains north of here for a few nights?"

I was completely overwhelmed! I looked bug-eyed at Skye and Addy for an answer, and of course, Skye spoke up immediately, "Whoa! That would be totally awesome! When do we leave?"

Looking at me, Luke asked, "What do you think, Leira? Do you want to rough it for a few days?"

I replied indignantly, "Of course I do. But, who else will be going?"

Luke answered, "Only me and the three of you."

Addy, apparently terrified at that idea, asked, "Shouldn't we have a grown-up with us? What happens if we get in trouble? What about snakes, insects and animals?"

Protectively, (because I was proud of my cousin and knew about his experiences in the wilderness) I calmly replied, "There's nothing to be worried about. I've already told you Luke is an Eagle Scout. Before we leave, I'll tell you about the incredible things he's done. Believe me, nothing bad will happen to us with Luke around. Just think of the adventures we'll have. Besides, he IS an adult, eighteen-years-old. Think of the awesome stories we'll have to tell everyone back home!"

I heard Addy mutter under her breath, "If we get back."

Actually, I was slightly nervous. But, I smiled cheerfully and asked, "Well, when do we leave, where are we going and what do we bring with us?"

Luke happily replied, "We'll be leaving in the morning as soon as everything is packed. We'll have some work to do tonight before you go back to your comfy hotel. We'll be traveling into the mountains and canyons of Sedona. It's roughly a two-hour drive. I've made up a list of things you'll need to bring." He handed each of us a paper, and as we perused it, he continued, "One thing you have to do before leaving tonight is to let me know what you don't have on the list. Any questions?"

Addy, Skye and I shook our heads no. Luke responded, "Well then, let's get started."

Luke left the room as the three of us looked over his lists. We were to check off what we already had. There were several ordinary items, like clothes, jackets for chilly nights and brushes for our hair and teeth. We were to wear sturdy sneakers or hiking boots. In addition, we needed backpacks. The three of us had the ones we used on the plane, so we checked that off. I finished checking my list, then I looked up at Skye and Addy and questioned, "Don't you think this list is kind of short? What about shampoo, conditioner, soap, sandals, suntan lotion, bug spray, and—more importantly—a camera?"

Skye replied, "Yeah. Let's go find Luke and ask him. We have everything else but sleeping bags. Hey, what about pillows? Those aren't written down either." We traipsed off in search of him.

Addy asked nervously, "Are you positive he knows what he's doing?"

I quickly responded, "Of course!" The first person we found was Uncle Ray, so we asked him where Luke might be.

He replied jovially, "Oh, he's probably in the garage getting out what you need for your trip."

The three of us hurried to the garage, and sure enough, he was there, pulling out an assortment of things. Walking up to him, I said, "We're finished with our lists, and the only thing we don't have are sleeping bags."

Climbing a ladder to reach a high shelf, he responded, "That's no problem. Here, catch." With that, he pulled down one sleeping bag at a time and threw them to us. I caught mine with a noisy, "Oomph!" Stifling a grin as he climbed down the ladder, Luke asked me, "Are you telling me cousin that all three of you have 'hiking' backpacks?"

Skye replied confidently, "We each brought one on the plane. They're our school packs, and they can sure hold a lot of heavy books."

Luke grinned and murmured, "Um…I figured that's what you had. Unfortunately, they are NOT appropriate for hiking and camping. Here, let me get you 'real backpacks'. Climbing back up the ladder, he pulled down four massive backpacks! Each one had two vertical metal rods for support.

Astonished, Addy asked, "These are backpacks? How are we supposed to carry them?"

Luke replied, "Your sleeping bag fits sideways across the top part of the pack. Then everything else goes inside."

"Slightly confused, I said, "But Luke, there's enough room to put everything on your list for all three of us in one pack. And what about the things you forgot to write down?"

He squinted, and then asked curiously, "What 'things' are you talking about?"

Addy stated seriously, "Well, first of all you didn't include our hair stuff, or even soap to wash with. And what about towels?"

Skye blurted out, "You didn't even put a pillow on the list, not to mention pajamas!"

I rapidly added, "And what about suntan lotion, bug spray, snacks and drinks? Oh and one more important thing, what are we going to eat for breakfast, lunch and dinner?"

"Hold on a minute." Luke replied. "First of all, take a look around you at what is laid out on the floor."

He gave us a few minutes to take in the sight. It included canteens, metal plates, eating utensils, cooking pans, sharp knives, an emergency kit, suntan lotion, bug towelettes, several cans of soup and other foods, as well as items that we couldn't identify. When we looked back up at him, he continued, "This is all we'll need for the three nights we're there. In addition to the items on your list, we will distribute these objects between us."

"To answer your question about the 'missing' items, let me say this. The backpacks will be full and heavy. You don't need any 'hair stuff' other than a brush and maybe a hair tie. There are not any showers in the canyons, and even if we happen upon a pond or small waterfall, we can't pollute them. I've brought along environmentally safe soap to wash our hands and faces as necessary. You don't need pajamas because you'll sleep in your clothes or underwear; whichever is more comfortable, depending upon the temperature. I'll be carrying a small pop-up tent for you and I'll sleep out in the open. If it rains—which it probably won't—I have a light waterproof piece of tenting that's easily propped up to cover me. There'll be no room for pillows. You can use your jacket or a piece of clothing to lay your heads on."

As he spoke, Skye, Addy and I listened intently with our jaws hanging open in astonishment, never making a peep.

Luke continued in a matter-of-fact tone, "In regards to food, I'm bringing enough cans of assorted stuff for three hearty lunches. Tomorrow, we'll bring sandwiches to eat after we set up camp. I'm bringing granola meal bars for breakfast. I've also packed trail mix in case anyone gets hungry between meals. As he paused, I calmly asked, "And what about supper?"

Luke responded enthusiastically, "Don't worry, I'm an excellent cook! So let's merely say that it's a surprise for now. I want to leave around seven in the morning, so Leira, have your mom get you here by five-thirty to have breakfast and be ready to go. I'll put your backpacks together tonight, minus your essential items. Any questions?"

Addy, Skye and I were speechless. Seeing the looks on our faces, Luke said reassuringly, "Look, I know this seems a bit scary to you, but I've done this at least fifty times. Leira, my parents and yours would never put you in any danger. It's true that we need to respect the desert and all of the life there. Through scouting, I've been trained to do things much more difficult than go on a camping trip. I've also been to this particular place several times because its beauty and history fascinates me. I know you'll love it too. At times, you might be a bit afraid, but remember, the three of you are best friends. In addition, Leira, I'm your cousin, and I love you like a sister. Just don't tell Mom or Dad I said that or I'll never live it down. Oh, and don't tell my sisters either." After a short pause, he asked, "Well, are you willing to go on an adventure or not? I don't want to spend the next three hours packing all of this stuff if you're going to chicken out."

Skye, who never wanted anyone to doubt her courage, replied enthusiastically, "I'm ready." Looking at Addy and I, she challenged, "What about you two?"

I gazed around at everything to be packed and said, "These backpacks might be quite heavy. Are you sure we can carry them?"

Luke replied, "Of course. I'm going to pack them according to what I believe each of you can handle. Remember, we only have to take them down once into the canyon. On the trip back up they'll be much lighter. If we have trouble traveling there or coming back, we can shift the weight, or if necessary, we can leave some things and go back for them. There's nothing to worry about. Besides, we're not on a strict time schedule, so if anyone needs rest, that will be fine."

I replied, "Ok, I'm ready to go." Then I looked at Addy. I could sense her apprehension and told her light-heartedly, "Addy, if you don't want to go, you don't have to." I looked over at Skye for agreement, and when she gave a slight nod, I continued, "We'll both understand." Feeling that Addy was still unsure, I added, "If you don't want Skye or me to go either, we promise not to be mad." Looking at Skye for conformation, she reluctantly said to Addy, "We're best friends. It's your decision."

Addy, as expected, rose to the challenge and replied, "Well, I went to Grimly Manor and its cemetery with both of you, and wonderful things happened, so I'm definitely not going to miss this adventure!"

Laughing, the three of us hugged one another. Then Luke interrupted us, "Leira, tell your mom we're going. You need to return to the hotel, pack up what's on your list, and be back here by five-thirty in the morning, so get going!"

When we arrived back at our hotel, Addy entered the room first and said in an anxious voice, "Someone has been here while we were gone. Look!" Gazing around, she continued, "The towels are all picked up!" Running into the bedroom area, she gasped, "Someone's made the bed!"

As she looked at us with a mixture of fear and amazement, I replied, "Addy, it's just the maids. This is a hotel. Every day, the maids come in and clean the room, make the bed, give us fresh towels and other things we've used up, like shampoo or soap."

A look of understanding and slight embarrassment crossed her face as she replied, "I didn't know that. I've never stayed at a place like this before."

Skye sympathetically said, "I know exactly how you feel because that's just what happened to me a few years ago when I first stayed at a hotel, so don't feel silly."

I added, "Forget about that. Let's just get our stuff together fast and get to sleep. We're definitely going to need it!"

Mom loudly added, "Everyone needs a quick shower before bed. Leira, you're first."

Although we complained the whole time, the three of us took short showers and packed up for our adventure. When my mom finally shut off the lights to go to sleep, I whispered to her, "Mom, are you worried about our trip?"

She replied softly, "Of course I am. I'm just one of those worrisome moms. However, one thing I'm sure of is that Luke is trustworthy, competent and a resourceful young man. You will be perfectly safe with him; otherwise, I wouldn't let you go!"

Chapter 6

Descent into the Canyon

The alarm clock went off at five o'clock the following morning. I don't think any of us slept well. Even Mom looked tired. We quickly got dressed, gathered our things and headed over to Aunt Debbie's house.

Luke answered the door when we arrived, wide-awake and grinning. I asked him, "How come you're not tired?"

He replied, "I slept great and I'm raring to go!"

Skye rolled her eyes and responded, "Oh brother."

Addy had an expression of delight on her face. She inhaled deeply and said, "Do you smell that? I think it's bacon, eggs and hash browns! Come on Leira; let's go see what your aunt has cooked up." As we rounded the corner into the kitchen, I saw that Addy was right.

Luke said, "The three of you should have a substantial breakfast. I've just finished mine. You'll probably want to take a nap during the drive to the canyon. You're going to need all of your energy today." We nodded as we began filling up our plates. Aunt Debbie had even made home-baked bread, onto which I heaped creamy, salted butter. The only sounds over the next several minutes were chewing, forks scraping plates and the garbled noises of contentment. After breakfast, we found Luke in the garage again. He had just finished packing. He glanced over at us and said, "Go say goodbye to everyone. We'll be leaving in a few minutes."

As I gave my mom a kiss and an enormous hug, we both said at the same time, "Don't worry." We chuckled, and I said, "I'll miss you, especially at night. I might even cry—as I did that year when I went off to Camp Good News."

Mom replied, "You'll be fine, and I'll worry enough for the both of us! Just pay attention to Luke and keep an eye on each other. Bring me back some exciting stories." I nodded and gave her another hug. Then we piled into Luke's rugged, mud-splattered jeep. As we were backing out of the driveway, we waved to Mom, Aunt Debbie, Uncle Ray, Tara, Brianna and Carrie (with Hannah asleep in her arms). They waved, shouting, "Have a great time!"

Luke described the area where we were going to camp. Within a half-hour, the three of us were sound asleep. We woke up abruptly as the jeep pulled onto a steep, rocky, dirt pathway. Startled, I asked, "What time is it? Where are we?"

Luke replied, "Well, you guys missed some spectacular scenery, especially in Sedona."

Skye groggily responded, "Huh, what? I thought we were going to Sedona."

Luke gave a short laugh and said, "We went through the most beautiful parts about fifteen or twenty minutes ago. I tried to wake you up, but no one answered, except with some loud snores! By the way, your snoring will help keep the animals away from camp during the night."

Addy immediately inquired, "What kind of animals?"

Luke replied, "I was trying to tell you about some of things to expect, but I guess my lively conversation put the three of you to sleep. While we're hiking down into the canyon, I'll teach you many things, so I don't expect anyone to fall asleep then! We'll be arriving at our parking area in a few minutes."

The jeep continued climbing upwards over unbelievably rocky paths. The jeep was rocking and bouncing so severely that we couldn't even talk to one another. Every time we hit an especially large bump, I thought it was going to roll over. It was nerve-wracking. I could tell by the expressions on their faces that Skye and Addy felt the same way. Several minutes passed and finally we came to a halt in a small dirt area off the rocky path. Luke looked back at us with a wide grin and asked, "Is everyone alright?"

Skye, looking a bit perturbed, answered, "Oh yeah. We're just fine, except for the bumps and bruises from bashing into Addy."

Luke laughed and replied, "Well then, let's get started. The real adventure is about to begin!"

Addy and I looked at one another suspiciously. Then I said to my cousin, "Luke, maybe we should go back towards the prettier part of Sedona and spend the night at that incredible B&B my mom took Aunt Debbie and me to. Then we could start off fresh tomorrow." I gave him my sweetest smile while Addy and Skye nodded enthusiastically.

Luke shook his head, and with a 'Yeah, right, I'm not falling for that one' expression, replied, "Let's get going. It is nine-thirty now, and if we pace ourselves, we will get to camp around noon."

"NOON?" Skye questioned. "Are you saying it's going to take 2 1/2 hours to get there?"

Luke casually replied, "Only if we get a move-on. Let's get the backpacks out, and I'll fit them on you."

He strapped mine on first. It was snug over my shoulders and felt a bit heavy, but I could handle it. Next, he attached my sleeping bag to the top of the pack, and then clipped on my canteen. The pack became much heavier after adding the additional items to it. Luke told me to sit down and wait until everyone else was fitted and handed me a frosty bottle of sports juice to drink.

I watched while Luke helped Addy next. She did not look very happy. I thought to myself, "Well, at least she doesn't look scared." When she was all set, she walked over to me. After sitting down, she asked, "Does yours feel too heavy?"

I replied, "A little. What about yours? Does it feel alright?"

She responded, "I guess I can get by—for a while anyway!" Addy and I sipped our drinks as Luke put on Skye's equipment. After finishing, she said suspiciously, "Hey, this looks bigger and heavier than theirs."

Luke answered, "I took height, weight and bone structure into consideration and adjusted the weight of the packs accordingly." Skye looked at him skeptically, and then glanced over at me with a look I interpreted as, "You're getting special treatment." I stood up, looked directly at Skye, and asked, "Do you want to transfer some things to me? I don't mind—really!"

A bit shamefaced she replied, "No, I'm OK. Let's go."

Luke piped in, "Skye, go have a cool drink and sit down until I'm ready." We watched in amazement as he outfitted himself. He loaded on at least three times as much as we were carrying, and he did it effortlessly and quickly. Once he was satisfied that everyone was all set, he locked up the jeep, and with a smile stated, "Follow me."

For the first twenty minutes or so, the descent wasn't too steep, but then it began to twist and deepen. As time passed, my backpack felt increasingly heavy. Each of us was concentrating so much on every step we took, that none of us uttered more than a slight gasp every so often. We were breathing a bit heavily when we came to a small level clearing near a much steeper incline, when Luke stopped us.

He said, "Let's all sit down and have a few sips of water. We'll rest here for about five minutes while I tell you a little about the plant life surrounding us."

Gazing around, we noticed many different types of flowers, plants and cactus.

Luke continued, "I want to educate you on the different types of cacti you see around us. The first thing I'm sure all of you realize is that each of these cacti has painful spines. You need to be very careful to avoid brushing against them while we're here."

Addy quickly asked, "Are they poisonous?"

Luke replied, "No, but depending upon which type you might get 'stuck' with; there are different types of treatment. But, none of them are worse than a pin prick, unless you get stuck in the eye."

All three of us inhaled repulsively, and then I asked, "Are you trying to scare us?"

Luke replied, "No, sorry. I was just trying to lighten things up a bit. I've never heard of such a thing happening—and—I don't ever want to!"

He stood up and walked over to a cactus plant with broad pancake-shaped segments. He motioned us to come closer, and then said, "These are prickly pear cacti, which you should consider as our friends—unless of course you whack one or sit on it. The prickly pear consists of these pads, (he pointed to the pancake parts), which are jointed together. When they break off, they form new plants. They are an excellent source of water, as are all cacti. They can also be cooked and eaten." Noticing our distaste, he hastily added, "They're actually quite tasty! I'm sure all of you will enjoy them. Also, the inner part can be used for treating cuts and burns."

Continuing, despite our skeptical looks, he moved over a bit to the right and pointed at a plant that looked as it was made of several long round hairbrushes. It was three to four feet high and covered with many bristles.

Luke informed us, "These buggers are everywhere and you obviously want to stay away from them. If you stumble into a prickly pear cactus, you may get a few spines stuck in you, but the small spines on these cholla cacti embed themselves into your skin at the slightest touch. If you look closely, you can see hundreds of small spines on each segment, and because they're so sticky, you can't pull them off with your hand. So, try to stay away from them. I'll tell you about the other cacti after we make this next descent. It should take about thirty minutes, but be careful and move slowly. The path is surrounded by chollas, and at one point there's a fairly steep drop off to the left."

Skye, Addy and I looked at one another nervously, but we got up and followed Luke. As we started the descent, he looked back at us and stated, "Hold the hand of the person in front of you. That way if any of you need to steady yourselves, there'll be someone to help you."

I was first in line after Luke, so I wasn't actually afraid, but I could see from Skye and Addy's expressions that they were. Feeling guilty, I called out to Luke, "Wait! I think when you see a good spot, then maybe we— meaning Skye, Addy and I—should switch places. I'm sure whoever is behind you will feel safer and, well, it's not fair if we don't change once in a while." I quickly eyed Addy and Skye and they both nodded their approval.

Luke said, "Sure, that's a good idea Leira." Then, we continued our descent. About half way down, we came to the spot on our left, with the terrifying drop-off that Luke had warned us about. Luckily, the trail wasn't too narrow, or I might not have gotten by it. Addy and Skye both grimaced as they glanced over the edge. We continued through and successfully made our way down. We switched places twice so each of us had equal time with Luke in the lead. Finally, we came upon another small spot to rest. I'm sure Addy and Skye were as grateful as I was because my backpack straps were starting to dig into my shoulders.

Once seated, Luke proceeded to tell us about the mighty Saguaro cactus, which could grow up to fifty feet high, and weigh nearly twenty-four thousand pounds! They could live up to two hundred years. There were so many of them in sight that I curiously asked, "Do they grow in other countries?"

Luke replied, "Actually, no, they don't. They only grow here in the Sonoran Desert. Don't you think that's kind of cool?" We all agreed with a nod as we sipped from our canteens. Luke continued, "I know your backpacks are feeling heavier, but the next half-hour won't be so difficult. Are you ready?"

I perceived slight nods from Skye and Addy and replied, "Just remember to change places every ten minutes or so. I think other than that we're OK." We paced ourselves over the next half hour and arrived at another stopping point. It was eleven o'clock and not only was the sun hotter, but I was getting hungrier.

Luke offered four snack bars from his pocket, which we gratefully accepted. He said in a serious voice, "Eat slowly and drink plenty of water. When we get to the base of this next descent, there is a clear spring where we can fill our canteens. This next stage will take us about another half-hour, and it's the steepest descent of our journey. We'll take it extremely slow and make sure you mind those cholla cacti. After that it's a fairly flat walk to our campsite."

Uplifted that we were nearing our camp, I concentrated on every footstep. We proceeded without mishap for about twenty minutes. Then, a small, but nasty accident occurred. Skye, who was last, stumbled while I was holding her hand and she let go of me. Her hand grabbed towards the nearest object, which was a prickly pear cactus. She cried out angrily as the spines penetrated her skin. Instantly, Luke, Addy and I halted. Luke quickly climbed the few yards up to her and examined her hand. There were six or seven spines embedded in it. Skye said bravely, "I'm OK. I'll just pull them out. It's nothing, really."

Luke responded, "You're a real trooper, but I have to take them out and put some antibiotic ointment on those punctures. Then, I'll cover your hand with a bandage." Skye nodded. It only took Luke a few minutes for us to be on our way again. I was relieved we only had about ten minutes left of the descent.

As we neared the level floor of the canyon, exhausted, I breathed an enormous sigh of relief. I sensed Skye and Addy felt the same way. Reaching level ground, I shouted, "Hurray! Can we take a break now?" I took two more quick steps and clumsily lost my balance. While falling, my arm brushed painfully across a cholla cactus! Luke, who had turned around at my 'hurray' rushed quickly to my side as I let out a screech. Tears started pouring from my eyes. I was in too much pain to feel embarrassed. Skye and Addy stood by helplessly while Luke worked his magic. He unhooked his backpack, took out an emergency kit and picked out a tiny comb. With tears still streaming down my face, I asked, "What's that?"

He replied, "It's an unusual comb to remove the spines. Just hold still." Trying not to make a fuss, I watched as he ran the comb down my arm and wiped it off on some kind of towelette. He did this several times until he was sure he had gotten all of them. Next, he applied a soothing antibiotic cream that stopped most of the stinging. He put everything away and asked, "Are you alright to continue, or do you want to rest a little more?"

Skye and Addy looked at me with concern, so I replied, "It's much better now. Thanks Luke. I was so stupid to take my mind off the trail when we reached the bottom."

Luke said sympathetically, "I've seen this happen more than once. What's most important is you're OK. Do you want to finish the last half hour to camp now, or rest? I can take your pack if you want."

I replied, "No, thanks. I'm fine. Let's just get going, because I'm starved!"

Addy and Skye agreed, and then we 'carefully' traipsed off after Luke. True to his word, within thirty minutes, we arrived at what he called 'base camp'.

Luke stated, "It's from here that we'll scout out a good place to set up camp." As he looked at the shock on our faces, he promptly added, "We're going to put our gear down now and find the perfect place to set up our tent.

Reading the looks of despair on our faces, he added, "Don't worry! It'll be close by—and we won't be carrying our packs." Seeing our looks of relief, he said, "We'll do our exploring from this area." It was an open spot with some plant life and scrub brush. The canyon walls—hundreds of feet away—were deep, but sloped backwards gently.

Luke helped us unhook our backpacks. Once they were off, the three of us sat down gasping, "Aww!" in relief.

While enjoying the rest, Luke said, "I'll let you guys catch your breath while I get the lunches my mom made for us."

Watching Skye close her eyes, Addy and I did the same while Luke set out a picnic of eight sandwiches, a large bag of chips, and four chocolate brownies. As we opened our eyes, hunger pangs returned sharply, and the four of us dug in. Having stuffed myself with Aunt Debbie's lunch, I reached for my canteen and realized it was empty. Glancing quickly at Skye and Addy, I knew they were also remembering that Luke had said the spring was at the base of the descent. Looking nervously at Luke, I asked, "Do we have to walk a half-hour back to get more water?"

He responded lightly, "No, there's another spring about fifty yards from here. Addy, since you're the only one uninjured among the three of you, how about grabbing Skye's canteen. I'll take Leira's, and we'll walk over and fill them up."

Addy cheerfully responded, "I better not catch you guys eating my second sandwich or my brownie!"

Laughing, Skye and I promised not to. We watched as they trekked the fifty yards or so to the spring, and continued to eat while they filled the canteens and returned. With full bellies, exhaustion started to creep up on my friends and me. Luke 'kindly' jerked us out of our peaceful frame of mind by loudly stating, "Okay! Let's set up camp!" Each of us let out an enormous groan.

Chapter 7

First Night in the Desert

Luke chuckled lightly as we groaned about pitching camp. We watched, slightly confused as he began pacing slowly throughout an ever-increasing area. Skye and I stood up and walked over to him. I asked, "What are you doing now? Are you making sure there's no cholla cacti for me to stumble into?"

Luke stopped, looked over at Addy and motioned for her to join us. When she reached us, he squatted down, and the three of us took his hint and crouched down near him.

After a slight hesitation, he said matter-of-factly, "Girls, I know you aren't familiar with the desert, and it's inhabitants, but I'm going to teach you over the next few days. The desert is NOT a terrible place. It's full of life and beauty."

"Before we set up camp, I'm going to scout an area from that Saguaro Cactus (he pointed towards one about three hundred yards away), to that one. (He pointed in the opposite direction at about the same distance).

What I'm looking for is the best and most advantageous spot to build the camp."

Addy inquired anxiously, "What do you mean by 'advantageous'?"

Luke responded, "There are many creatures that inhabit the desert, including insects, scorpions and snakes."

Our jaws dropped! Luke quickly added, "It's likely we'll run into all of them during our explorations, but (he held up his hand to halt our questions), I assure you that you'll be perfectly safe at all times. I need you to trust me. Tarantulas –"

I burst out, "TARANTULAS, as in SPIDERS?"

Luke continued with a smile, "Yes, spiders are common in the desert. Tarantulas may look very scary, but it's rare for them to bite someone unless they're provoked. As long as you walk away, there's no problem. In fact, many people keep tarantulas as pets. In all my years scouting, I've never seen anyone bit by one. Even if that did happen, it would only cause mild swelling and irritation. If you see one near the camp and you're afraid, just let me know, and I'll remove it. Any questions now?"

Skye asked sarcastically, "What if one creeps up on our sleeping bag at night? Somehow, I don't think we'd calmly get up and walk away."

Luke replied, "Every night before you zip yourselves in, I'll examine everything in the tent. Spiders and snakes can't enter after you've zipped your tent closed. You'll be perfectly safe."

Alarmed, Addy questioned, "Snakes? What kind of snakes?"

Luke replied, "There are several different types of snakes here. A snake is almost never aggressive. They only strike if they feel threatened. I'll always be in the lead during our walks. Each of us will find our own 'walking stick' to use, not only to sweep our pathways clear for us, but also to help us with any climbing we might do. While I'm scouting for the best area to set up the tent, you can follow me and search for decent sticks. Look for a sturdy stick that reaches above your hips or higher—as we can always cut it down. Let me know if you find one."

We started in a southerly direction towards the first Saguaro cactus.

Luke continued, "The snake that requires the most respect here is the Western Diamondback Rattlesnake. It's also commonly known as the 'King of the Southwestern Rattlers'." Noticing our complexions turn pale, he quickly added, "They hunt mostly at night. Believe me, if we do happen upon one during the day, it'll let us know by its extremely loud rattle. Actually they're quite beautiful, especially the ones that are pinkish in color. They have dark diamond shapes along their backs, and their heads have two dark stripes that make them look like they're wearing a black mask."

I said, "I'd rather not see the snake even if you think it's beautiful." Addy nodded in agreement, but Skye asked, "Luke if you see one, can you make sure I take a picture of it? That would be awesome! No one at home will believe it!"

Luke nodded his head and smiled. Then, he bent down and picked up a long, thick stick. He said with satisfaction, "This is a perfect walking stick, but I think it's just a little short for me."

Skye asked, "How tall are you?"

He replied, "Almost six feet, but I think this is the perfect height for you Skye. You're about five feet tall, right?"

As he handed it over to her, she replied smiling, "I'm exactly five feet." Then she tried the stick out with a sweeping motion and said, "I think it's just right for keeping snakes and tarantulas out of my way, but I can't be sure about the climbing part."

I noticed that while Skye was speaking to Luke, her face looked slightly flushed. Curiously, I asked, "Skye, are you getting a sunburn?"

She answered, "No, I don't think so. Why?"

I replied, "I thought you looked a bit pink, but it's gone now. Maybe it was the way the sun was reflecting off the canyons." I noticed her face reddening again and then it hit me like a ton of bricks; Skye liked Luke! Not wanting to embarrass her, I said to Luke, "Let's just keep going so we can get camp set up." Glancing at my watch, I exclaimed, "It's already three o'clock!"

About halfway to the Saguaro cactus, Luke stopped, bent over and picked up another longer, hefty stick. He swung it around and said, "This one's mine. It's even got a crook at the top, for a handle."

I asked, "Why didn't you just include walking sticks on your lists?"

He responded, "I find it more interesting to find the sticks along the way."

This time, Addy rolled her eyes and said, "Oh brother."

Luke looked back towards where we had left our gear and said confidently, "Follow me. I've found the best place to pitch camp." On the walk back, I picked up a stick. Handing it to Luke, I inquired, "Do you think this one is right for me?" He held it up, tested its weight, and while handing it back to me, replied; "I think this one will do nicely for you Leira."

We continued to retrace our steps. About halfway back, Luke stopped and pronounced, "Camp!"

I asked, "Why here?"

He replied, "I haven't seen a snake, tarantula or scorpion between the place we dropped off our gear and where we turned back." He punched his stick into the ground like a flag, and told us to go get our stuff.

The four of us retrieved our packs and returned to the spot Luke had designated. After telling us to place our things about ten feet away from the center, he proceeded to remove the tent from his gear. I looked at Skye and Addy and asked softly, "Do you think this will take a long time, like when my dad set up the tent in my backyard for our sleepover?"

Skye replied, "I doubt it; look how small it is. I don't think it's possible for the three of us to even sleep in it."

We watched nervously as Luke removed the outer cover and placed it on the ground. The tent began to spring to life! Within a minute, it was finished! Astonished, I stuttered, "That's impossible!"

Skye whispered in awe, "I don't believe it."

Luke smiled knowingly and replied, "This is what you call a 'Quick Set -Up Dome Tent'."

Addy gasped, "Wow, that's incredible! It's so much bigger than I thought it would be. I can't believe it fit in that small pack."

Luke replied, "It weighs fourteen pounds and will withstand any rain that probably won't come our way." He pointed out the two doors and one window. Then, he showed us what he called a 'rain fly'.

Skye quickly asked, "What the heck is a rain fly?"

Luke replied, "It acts as an umbrella for the tent should it rain extra hard." Then he pulled a similar piece of material out of his hiking pack and said, "This is a second rain fly I can erect above my sleeping bag if it does happen to rain."

The three of us stood there shaking our heads in wonder. Then I asked, "Okay, what's next?"

While laying the rain fly out on the ground, Luke replied, "Unload your packs. Along with your sleeping bags, place any personal articles or clothing in the two storage pockets inside the tent. Put any other items from your pack on the rain fly for me to deal with."

As we were unpacking, I noticed Addy glancing around. Her mind was obviously on more than the task at hand. I whispered to her, "Addy, what's wrong? What are you looking for?"

Her face reddened considerably as she quietly replied, "I'm looking for snakes, scorpions and tarantulas, but most of all, I have to go to the bathroom. I'm too embarrassed to ask—and—I'm afraid of the answer."

I replied sympathetically, "Well, I have to go too." Taking a deep breath, I continued, "I'll ask the question since he's my cousin. Don't feel bad; I'm embarrassed too."

Hesitantly, I walked over to Luke shuffling the sand beneath my shoes. With my eyes cast downwards, I said to him, "Um, Luke…?" Grimacing, I was suddenly at a loss for words. Luke squinted at me and questioned softly, "What is it Leira?"

I tried again, "Luke, Addy and I need to, um…."

Luke held up his hand, to silence me and asked knowingly, "Do you need to use the facilities?"

I looked up nervously and nodded my head. Considering how he had phrased the question, I queried back, "Do we have facilities?"

He grinned, walked over to his pack, and pulled out two items: a thick piece of plastic and a small stack of paper stuff. He held them out to me and said, "The facilities are all around us, and this (unfolding the plastic piece) is the privacy sheet." Handing me the other stack, he continued, "These are the wipes. They are biodegradable, meaning nature will absorb them. Choose a spot where you feel comfortable and have one of your friends hold up the sheet while you do your business. OK?"

Blushing, I accepted both items and replied, "Alright." I took 'the necessities' over to Addy and Skye. Apparently, they'd overheard the conversation. Without any further word, the three of us headed off towards a relatively secluded area, but within sight of Luke and the camp. None of us wanted to be out of shouting distance in case we saw a critter we were afraid of. All three of us took our opportunity at that point, so we could stay together. Relieved at last, we hurried back to camp to finish unpacking. As we entered the tent, we were surprised at its spaciousness. It easily fit our unrolled sleeping bags with enough room in the storage pockets for most of our clothing. Outside the tent, we looked at the assortment of items spread over the rain fly. I asked, "Wow—did we carry all of that?"

Luke replied encouragingly, "Yes, we did! It's everything we'll need." He started naming obvious things like metal pans, utensils and a collapsible grill. He had also brought many cans of foodstuff. I presumed they were for lunch and dinner, but it didn't seem like nearly enough. Then I noticed two canvas bags that were empty and asked, "Luke, what are they for?"

Luke replied, "One is for trash that we'll have to carry back. The other is for food storage. We'll need to hang it up on that tree (pointing to our left) to protect it from possible—but unlikely predators."

Addy and I cried in unison, "Predators?"

Skye inquired hesitantly, "Predators? Do you mean snakes and such?"

Luke studied us while considering his answer, and then said, "Coyotes are indigenous to the desert." Addy started to interrupt, but Luke stopped her and stated firmly, "Let me finish before any of you ask more questions, please."

All three of us nodded our heads. Luke continued, "Coyotes are predators, but they rarely come within the range of humans, especially when they have enough water and food. You'll probably hear them howl occasionally in the evening, but that's nothing to worry about. That's just their way of communicating to each other. They also bark, yelp and huff. I'm familiar with all of their sounds. The best thing to do is enjoy their beautiful music." Raising his left brow and giving a lopsided grin he added, "That's what most westerners have done for a few hundred years. Any questions?"

Addy tentatively asked, "Well, no, not about the coyotes, but you said, 'predators', plural. What other ones are there?"

Luke inhaled a deep breath, and replied, "On VERY rare occasions you'll hear the piercing screech of a Mountain Lion." Luke held up his hand once again to stop any retort. "I've only experienced this three times' in the fifteen or so times I've camped here. If we hear one and you're too afraid, then we can pack up and move camp or go home. Your safety is more important than anything else, and I hope, in the end that you'll remember this as a fantastic adventure. So, any other questions?"

Skye replied, "Yeah! When do we eat? I'm starved!"

Addy and I looked at one another, and I asked her, "Well, do you have any questions for Luke?"

Wide-eyed, she answered, "No. I trust Luke…. I guess, and I'm hungry too."

I looked at my watch, then at Luke, and replied, "OK, I guess our only question is 'when do we eat'?"

Luke laughed and said, "As soon as I've heated up the slop."

The three of us looked at him in shock! Laughing again, he asked, "How do hotdogs, beans and potato chips sound?"

I grimaced, and replied, "It sounds tasty, but the three of us have to sleep in the same tent, which might get a bit stinky."

Luke laughed and said, "Well, it's a lucky thing that I get to sleep out in the open air!"

We ate everything in sight, even though none of us liked baked beans. We were so famished we didn't complain. It had taken us a while to prepare the food.

Afterwards, Luke gathered up the rest of the food, tied it up in a canvas bag, and then hoisted it up the tree. He sent us to the small spring to wash our utensils and refill our canteens. Dusk had settled in when we realized how late it was. Luke made a complete search of our tent. When he finished, we crawled in and rolled down our sleeping bags. The only one of us that had brought pajamas was Addy, but at the last minute she decided that she'd rather be partially dressed if we needed to run!

Luke tended the remains of the fire while the three of us drifted off to sleep. We were too exhausted to worry. I wasn't sure if I was awake or dreaming when I heard the distant screech of a Mountain Lion. Half opening my weary eyelids, I listened for a moment more, and then fell deep asleep.

Chapter 8

Petroglyphs, Pictographs and Pemmican

Early the next morning I awoke to the delicious aroma of sizzling bacon. As the smell drifted through my senses, I abruptly remembered where we were. Immediately, I woke up Skye and Addy. Even though they were a bit groggy from sleep, they also perked up when they caught the scent of breakfast cooking. I unzipped the tent cautiously and peeked out. Luke was frying the bacon in a pan to the left of me. Before I had a chance to say anything, he saw me and said, "Morning campers! Are you ready for breakfast?"

I replied, "We'll be out in a few minutes."

He responded, "Don't wait too long or I'll eat all of this bacon myself."

I replied, "We'll be out in less than a minute!" Skye and Addy were almost dressed before I had a chance to grab my clothes. As they hurried out of the tent, I yelled to them, "Leave some for me!" I quickly pulled on a clean shirt, shorts, socks and shoes and headed outside with my brush in hand. Luke handed me a plate of steaming bacon, a breakfast bar and my canteen. He said, "Enjoy the bacon, there won't be any more until we get home."

We ate every nibble. Afterwards, I found the privacy sheet and Addy, Skye and I headed off to the designated spot. Skye and I had done our business, and Addy was about to begin when she screamed, "A SCORPION!" She rushed out from behind the plastic sheet heading straight for camp (luckily still clothed), with Skye and I trailing close behind! Luke heard the screams and had his stick and knife ready when we reached him.

Breathlessly, Addy gasped, "A scorpion—I almost sat on a scorpion."

Luke asked calmly, "Who would like to show me where the scorpion is?" Addy was shaking her shoulder-length blackish hair so fast that her features were a blur. Skye took one glance at her, and then tentatively replied, "I will. Leira, you stay here with Addy." I nodded. Skye walked towards the area, slowing down, as she got closer. Peering down to try and find it, Skye jumped a foot back and shouted, "There it is!"

Luke sprang forward, then, came to a sudden halt! He took a step backwards and called loudly over his shoulder, "Leira, Addy, come here. It's all right. It's not a scorpion." He could sense our reluctance, so he spoke firmly. "Both of you get over here now!"

As we approached, Luke pointed out 'the scorpion'. He stated simply, "This is not a scorpion, and it's not poisonous. It's commonly called a Wind spider, Camel spider or Wind scorpion. They move remarkably fast. Watch." He moved his stick near to it and it seemed to vanish!

He continued, "Actually they're very nice to have around the house. They kill and or eat smaller insects—including black widow spiders. It's gone now. Addy, you can finish up." Then Luke casually walked away. Addy motioned us to a different area, carefully checking it out. I noticed Luke back at camp preparing for the days adventure. When we returned, he stated, "Addy, you and Leira bring any washable items down to the spring along with this soap. Wash and dry them, then place them in this sack with the other items. Skye, you help me package up any leftover food.

Then I'll show you how to hang them from that tree so animals can't get them."

Skye blushed slightly. A tiny smile crossed her face. Then, she raised her brows and hesitantly asked, "Like you did last night?" Luke nodded with a slight grin.

After Addy and I had finished our chores, I asked Luke, "What about our sleeping bags and clothes?"

He replied, "That's a good question, Leira. Watch carefully and follow along." He laid out the rain fly and picked up his sleeping bag, motioning for us to do the same. As Luke opened his, he scanned it and methodically ran his stick and hands from one end to the other. Following his lead, we did the same. When Luke was convinced we had done the job to his satisfaction, we rolled our bags up tightly. Afterwards, I looked at Luke curiously and asked, "Why are we rolling them up when we're going hiking?"

He gave me a sly grin and replied, "Where we're going, there's a slight possibility that a storm might roll through. If that happens, we'll be prepared to spend a few hours or even the night someplace dry."

Seeing the fear cross our faces, he reassuringly said, "It's unlikely, and the bags only weigh five pounds each. It's better being safe than sorry. Besides, there's very little else to carry, and the plan is to be back here for dinner. Now, grab your sticks, canteens and your small shoulder packs and let's be off."

As we began hiking, Luke told us he was taking us to view ancient pictographs and petroglyphs. He explained, "Pictographs are extremely old symbols or images painted on rock walls. Petroglyphs are incised or scratched into the surface of the rocks."

After several more minutes of hiking, Skye inquired, "What's so exciting about these petro-whatevers? Why are we bothering to hike—and how long until we see them?"

Luke replied with a question, "Skye, do you know anyone who has seen a painting or inscription that's about three to eight thousand years old?"

The three of us looked at Luke in disbelief. Skye responded after a moment, "No! Are you telling me we're REALLY going to see something that old?"

Luke replied confidently, "Absolutely. More importantly, we're also going to see ancient cliff dwellings of the Sinagua Indians. I'll explain more after we hike up a few more trails."

Addy inquired, "What time are we going to stop for lunch? Oh, by the way, did you pack our lunch?"

Luke smiled and replied, "We'll stop about halfway to the cliff dwellings and feast on Native American treats, washed down with fresh spring water!"

Apprehensively, we gazed at one another, wondering what the 'treats' were. Hiking up a slightly steep incline, we paused at a small plateau where we quenched our thirsts from the canteens. I checked my watch and realized we had been hiking for over an hour. That surprised me a bit. After our short break, we continued up a steeper climb with deep drop-offs to our right. It was a little scary. It was at that point that we truly appreciated our walking sticks. We were also thankful that there were no tortuous cacti in our path. Exhausted, we reached another plateau and rested. Luke explained, "This area is near the ancient cliff dwellings of the 'Sinagua Indians' and the well of 'Montezuma'. I'm not an expert by any means, but I do know a bit about the history of the region. After we finish our lunch, I'll take you a little ways to show you the drawings."

I asked nervously, "Luke, you said we would have 'Native American treats'. What exactly does that mean?"

Luke shrugged off his backpack and removed what looked like strips of bacon. He handed each of us a piece and said enthusiastically, "Pemmican!"

Skye grimaced and asked, "What the heck is 'pemmican'? It sounds like Pelican."

Luke laughed, and explained, "Pemmican is mostly, dried ground up meat, mixed with dried berries and held together with animal fat. It's like beef jerky except it's slightly sweet because of the berries. Try it. It's fantastic! Oh, by the way, if you're out of water, there's a fresh spring right over there."

He pointed at a spot about fifty yards away where we could see the glistening water of a small spring. Then he happily began chewing on his pemmican.

With a shared grimace, we grabbed a strip of pemmican and began chewing. We were so hungry that it didn't taste so bad. After filling our canteens, we followed Luke down an incline that wasn't too steep, but perilous due to the numerous cacti.

We veered off the beaten path for five minutes or so and finally halted at what appeared to be nothing but a sheer cliff above us. Luke gazed at us with awe and delight, and then asked, "Can any of you see what is here?"

I gazed around searching for something—anything. Then, I looked at Addy and Skye for help. Their gazes were as blank as mine were. Embarrassed, I turned to Luke and said, "I have no idea what you're talking about."

Gazing at my friends, I noticed Skye blushing uncontrollably, and I realized that she didn't want to look stupid in front of Luke. So, I turned to Luke and asked in exasperation, "Are we going to stand here all day or are you going to tell us what we're supposed to be looking at?"

I thought he might be angry at the way I asked him, but once he began his explanation, I realized he was actually happy.

He pointed out subtle faint drawings and inscriptions. The pictographs and petroglyphs were almost invisible unless you knew what to look for. As we got our cameras out of our packs and began taking pictures, Luke explained how old they were and how they were created. As comprehension dawned on us, we began to appreciate what we were seeing. Luke answered every question easily, and it became obvious how captivated he was by the subject. After spending about an hour at the wall, I asked him, "What about the Cliff Dwellings? Are they far away? Can we see them before we go back?"

Luke considered my question for a moment before he finally responded, "Well, it's a little after three o'clock now, and the cliff dwellings are more than a half-hour away. If you want to see them today, we'll have to get going now, and we won't have much time to see them before we have to head back. It's up to the three of you. But, if we do go there, it's possible we'll have to spend the night in the open. So, go have a 'pow-wow', and let me know what you want to do."

As Skye, Addy and I discussed investigating the cliff dwellings, I was sure I had them convinced to keep going. Suddenly, Addy's eyes lit up like fireworks, and she covered her mouth in a soundless scream as she pointed a trembling finger toward the lowering afternoon sun. Looking in the direction she indicated, I saw a large BEAR lurking about two hundred yards away. I edged soundlessly over the few feet to Luke and linked my arm around his, for reassurance.

At the same time, Skye grabbed Addy, holding a hand over her mouth, quietly walked her backwards towards Luke and I.

Luke, who had seen the bear, said calmly, "We're going to slowly and quietly back down towards the plateau. It's only a black bear, so there's nothing to worry about, but it's best to be cautious."

Slightly calmed by Luke's assurance, we backed down the incline. We hung onto each other for dear life and kept glancing back to make sure he wasn't following us. During the hike, Luke tried relieving our fears by explaining that black bears are vegetarians and only known to lash out when it's a female with cubs. He said, "The one we just saw was a male. Believe me, he's much more afraid of us then we are of him." The walk seemed at first to take longer, but as we progressed, time seemed to speed up a bit. Finally, we reached the first plateau and Luke asked, "It's dusk, so do you want to stay here or go back to camp? If you want to continue and we travel relatively quickly, we should be back in thirty-to-forty minutes. What do you want to do?"

Looking at my best friends, I inquired, "What do you want?"

Addy replied, "Let's get back to camp now!"

I looked expectantly at Skye, and she replied, "I agree. Let's get going."

Luke said, "OK. Follow me, and if anyone has trouble—yell, whistle or whatever."

We followed Luke closely. The sun had set by the time we arrived. My stomach began to rumble from hunger. I think we all hoped Luke had something more filling and tasty than pemmican for dinner.

Luke lit a lantern and told us to unpack, get our sleeping bags set up, and to make sure we zipped up the tent when we were inside. We emerged from the tent to find Luke had already gotten a cooking fire blazing. We watched as he started frying up what looked like some kind of patties, and in another pan—beans.

Addy demanded, "Not BEANS again?"

Luke smiled, "These are Leira's favorite beans. They're lima beans."

I looked at Luke skeptically and said, "Well, yeah, I do like lima beans. But, I don't think I've ever had them fried before, and, what kind of burgers are those?"

Luke gleefully answered, "Your favorite! Chick Patties." Smiling, I replied, "Awesome! You definitely got that right. Thanks."

Along with the patties and beans, we also had some fresh nuts and berries that Luke had packed. Overall, it had been an adventurous day, especially the bear part. I was looking forward to writing about it in my journal.

After dinner, Luke instructed us to take the flashlight and wash the dishes in the stream while he cleaned up camp and inspected our bedding once again. As we approached the stream, Skye's flashlight reflected on a strange arrangement of sticks and stones, which we hadn't noticed before. Addy, who was behind us, bumped into me and said, "Sorry." Then sensing our nervousness, inquired, "What is it?"

As I fixed my flashlight on the strange configuration, I asked anxiously, "Do either of you remember these being here before?" Addy and Skye took a long look at it and then Skye replied, "No. Do you think we missed seeing it?"

Addy replied, "I have a pretty decent memory and we've been to this spot more than a few times. I'm pretty sure this wasn't here before."

I crept closer with my flashlight in hand. Aghast, I whispered, "LOOK! There aren't only sticks and stones placed here. If you look closely, you'll see markings engraved on some of them." We turned and raced back to camp—leaving the cooking pans and utensils behind—shouting, "Luke! Luke! Come here quick!"

Chapter 9

Night Two—Strange Signs

Luke had just finished checking our tent when he heard our cries. Quickly, he called out, "What's going on?"

I replied breathlessly, "Luke, someone has been in our camp! We saw a strange arrangement of sticks and stones that wasn't there before. And not only that! Something was painted and scratched into them. Quick! Follow us." As I turned around to run back, Addy stopped me in my tracks by shouting, "Leira!"

Looking slightly embarrassed, she continued, "I'm going to wait here." Glancing from me to Skye, she added quietly, "If that's OK."

Skye taunted her, "It's fine with me, but remember; you'll be all alone—unless that bear has followed us."

Addy glared at Skye and angrily replied, "That's not funny!"

As I was about to step in to try and smooth out the situation, Luke interrupted and said gently, "There's nothing to worry about. Everyone needs to take a deep breath and let it out slowly. After you have calmed down, we'll go together and check out what you've seen. Bring along your flashlights and walking sticks. Also, (gazing at our empty hands) I notice you've forgotten our pans and utensils. We need to pick them up, unless you REALLY want to get back to basics. Any questions?"

Skye looked a bit shame-faced and Addy a little upset, but we nodded our heads in acknowledgement. Luke took the lead with me beside him. Addy and Skye were right on our heels. When we reached the stream, we shined our lights on the strange arrangement. As I started to ask a question, Luke raised his hand for silence. All three of us crept near him as he crouched down and thoughtfully perused what we had discovered. Skye couldn't contain herself and blurted out, "What is it? Do you know?"

Once again, Luke held up his hand for silence. After studying the configuration for several moments, he got up and said in a quiet voice, "You're not in any danger but don't move. I just want to examine the ground around here without any more disturbances to the surroundings. Just give me a few minutes." Reluctantly, we nodded our heads. Luke walked slowly several yards in all directions from the arrangement. While scouring the area, I could tell he was trying to work something out. Finally, he crouched down near us and said, "This has undoubtedly been placed here since we left this morning. It's my opinion, that other hikers, or maybe just one, have come through this area. I think they wanted to spook us by leaving this here, where they knew we would find it. Most likely, they've gone home for the night, or there would have been signs of people carrying hiking and camping equipment."

Luke continued, "I don't see any need for concern, so let's get back to camp and get some sleep. Don't forget to take the pans and utensils."

Addy asked tentatively, "Are you sure?"

Luke replied, "If I wasn't, we would pack up camp and head back home." Addy breathed a sigh of relief and whispered, "I wish my puppy Katie was here with us. She'd let us know if there was someone around."

Skye and I nodded in agreement. Luke—having clearly heard us—replied, "If Katie was here, I'd be more worried about coyotes or mountain lions coming after her."

All three of us gasped in horror! Realizing his poor choice of words, Luke added, "Sorry, I didn't mean to frighten you. That was the last thing I should have said to set your mind at ease for the night." When we reached camp, Skye and Addy headed straight into the tent. As Skye was about to zip the tent closed, she asked me, "Leira, aren't you coming to bed now?"

Pensively, I replied, "Not right now. I want to talk to Luke for a few minutes. You can zip up the tent. I'll make sure it's closed tight after I crawl in."

Skye hesitantly replied, "Alright, but are you sure you don't want us to wait up?"

I tried to make my response sound casual, "No, I'm fine. I just want to talk with Luke for a while. I'm not tired after all of the excitement. You guys can go to sleep now. I'll be in before you know it." Skye zipped the tent shut and I was alone with Luke, sitting by the warm campfire.

Gazing thoughtfully at the fire, Luke looked over at me and whispered, "Do you want a snack?"

I questioned softly, "What kind of snack?"

Luke chuckled softly and replied, "A chocolate chip granola bar." Then he added, "You're getting too smart for me if you have to ask that. You waited until lunch before asking what 'Native American Treats' were."

I smirked and whispered back, "I'd love a granola bar, but after that, I want to know what you really think about what we saw. I have a feeling you're not telling us everything."

Luke reached over to his backpack and pulled out a few treats. As we munched on them, he said, "I've got to hand it to you cousin, you're pretty intuitive. I hope you're as brave if you want to help me solve this mystery." He looked at me with an intensity I'd never seen before. It felt like he was actually challenging me to step up to the task while keeping my mouth shut, or go to bed and forget we ever had this conversation.

With a bravado, I didn't know I possessed I replied softly, "I want to help." After a deep breath, I asked, "What do we have to do?"

After studying my face, Luke replied thoughtfully, "It's not that awful. I just want to scout around the perimeter of the encampment to see if there are more signs. Are you alright with that?"

I answered, "Yeah, but only if it's safe to leave Skye and Addy here alone." Luke assured me that we wouldn't be that far from camp and that the tent would always be within flashlight view.

I responded, "Okay then. Let's go." With the fire burning brightly to ward off animals, we headed off to the northeastern part of the camp with flashlights and sticks to guide our way. Luke was leading, and I was a half-step behind. After several minutes, Luke stopped abruptly! Bumping into him, I looked up and saw his light shining on another arrangement of sticks, and methodically placed stones. As he knelt closer, I crouched near him to get a better look. Once again, there were markings on the stones. I whispered nervously, "Luke, do you know what it means?"

Luke inhaled sharply—as though he'd figured something out. Then, he responded, "Leira, these two signs show me that someone with advanced knowledge of local Indian lore is trying to shake us up. I still believe whoever it was, has gone now."

Nervously, I asked, "How do you know they're not still here?"

Eventually, he replied, "It's hard to explain about everything I've learned about this environment and the people who lived here. The quickest answer I can give is that I recognize some of the symbols and believe whoever put them here doesn't mean us any harm."

I asked quickly, "Which symbols? And what do they mean?"

"Well", he thoughtfully replied, "This one." With his finger, he traced an 'S' shaped drawing with lines sketched across the top, bottom and sides. Then said, "I think this shape depicts a snake and the four lines surrounding it represent a barrier. If I'm correct, it's a symbol of protection."

I looked at him a bit skeptically as he continued, "I also think that we'll find more of these arrangements if we go to the northwestern and southwestern points of the camp. Do you want to come with me or go back?" As he waited patiently for my answer, he added, "Somehow, I don't think either of your friends would take this as calmly as you. What do you want to do?"

After carefully thinking over his comments, I stated, "I can deal with being scared, but only if you're really sure nothing bad will happen." I looked at him expectantly for his response.

Seriously, Luke replied, "I would die before I would ever let anything bad happen to you or your friends."

I replied, "Let's go." Then I shined my flashlight back towards the tent to make sure everything was quiet back at camp. We easily found the last two configurations surrounding the area. Investigating the last one, I asked Luke, "Are they all the same or different? I've been so afraid that I can't remember what each one looked like."

Luke gave my question some thought, and replied, "Each configuration is unique, but some of the drawings and inscriptions are similar. Whoever made them knows the symbolism of the Cliff Dwellers who lived here a long time ago. Unfortunately, without my computer I can't say exactly what they mean. From what I can remember, I don't believe the signs are threatening. Let's go back to camp now. In the morning, I'll take pictures of each location. Hopefully, when we get back home, I can use the Internet to figure it all out."

When we arrived at the tent, I looked at Luke nervously and asked one final time, "You're sure we're safe tonight, right?"

I thought Luke would scoff at me for asking such a question, but he looked me directly in the eye and replied, "If I didn't think it was ninety-nine point nine percent safe, I would be packing now. Don't ask me again or we're heading home. Go to bed. I'll stay awake for a while and stoke the fire."

Sarcastically, with a raised brow, I asked, "Ninety-nine point nine percent?"

He grinned, chuckled and replied, "Don't worry Leira, and sleep soundly. Tomorrow we're going to have another exhausting but adventurous day—and no bacon to start it off with!"

Glancing back at Luke with a small smile, I unzipped the tent, ducked inside and quickly zipped it closed. I knew I was putting on a decent show of bravery, but inside I was terrified. My eyes were heavy as I crept silently to my sleeping bag and slid into it. Then, I zipped the bag up to my chin, still wearing all of my clothes except my shoes. Little did I realize that exhaustion and fear had overwhelmed me, and before I knew it, I was sound asleep. I found out in the morning that the howling of coyotes had awakened Skye in the middle of the night, and even though she had tried to rouse me, my sleep was not disturbed.

Chapter 10

Indian Lore

Addy shook me awake early the next morning. She didn't have an easy time of it, but finally I groggily asked, "What? Let me go back to sleep."

Addy nudged me harder and loudly said, "Leira, wake up! I need to go to the bathroom, and I'm not going alone."

Yawning, I replied irritably, "Well, wake up Skye, she'll go with you. I'm going back to sleep." But, Addy pushed me again, harder, and stated irritably, "I've tried waking up Skye, but I think she's dead! So WAKE UP!"

I suddenly felt wide-awake. Quickly unzipping my sleeping bag, I asked urgently, "What do you mean? You're not serious, are you? What's wrong with her?" Hurrying to get out of my sleeping bag, my zipper caught on my clothes. I groaned in frustration as I looked up at Addy, waiting for an answer. Finally, Addy said, "Well, I might have exaggerated a little, but I really can't wake her up."

Releasing myself from the confines of my sleeping bag, I crawled over to Skye. I breathed a sigh of relief after seeing her chest rise and fall, and began shaking her and calling her name. Luke had apparently heard the ruckus and called through the tent, "Is everything all right in there?"

At that instant, Skye's eyes shot open, and she yelled out, "Stop it!" I could hear Luke unzipping the tent. I shouted to him that everything was fine, and we'd explain in a few minutes. Looking back at Skye, I said quietly, "You scared us half to death. You wouldn't wake up."

Skye looked up at us. Her green eyes were bloodshot. After letting out an enormous yawn, she replied in annoyance, "I only got a couple hours of sleep last night because of those rotten coyotes! Apparently, neither of you had any problem sleeping right through their howling! Now, can I go back to sleep?" At that, she promptly threw the top of her sleeping bag over her head.

Addy dragged the cover back off and responded fiercely, "No! You can't go back to sleep. What about the coyotes? How many do you think there were? Were they really close?"

Realizing that she wasn't going back to sleep, Skye grumpily sat up rubbing the sleepy-bugs from her eyes. After a moment or two, she squinted over at Addy and said, "They weren't that close, but they were VERY loud. Why don't you ask Luke and let me wake up when I'm ready?"

Addy scratched her cheek and looked back at me. I could see her noticing what I was wearing. Curiously, she asked, "Leira, why are you already dressed and how come you're still wearing your hiking clothes from yesterday? What's going on?"

I responded a bit sheepishly, "Well, I stayed up a little late last night with Luke, and I was too tired to change, that's all."

Skye looked at me suspiciously and said, "I thought you were just going to be a few minutes." Addy's dark eyes darted back and forth between Skye and me, anxiously waiting for my response.

I kept my eyes averted while chewing on my lower lip. Finally, I glanced up and replied, "Oh, all right. I stayed up longer than I thought I would because Luke and I checked out some areas of the camp looking for more signs or symbols like the ones we found earlier."

Both Addy and Skye shouted, "YOU WHAT?" As I was about to explain what happened, Luke demanded, "Everyone is to come out of the tent, now! Is that clear?"

All three of us grimaced in shock at the tone of his voice. We knew we'd better follow his orders. I called, "We'll be right out Luke." We saw his shadow move away as Addy and Skye tugged on their clothes and I unzipped the tent and headed outside.

Pandemonium struck as Luke simply asked us, "What happened in there?" All three of us started talking at once. Apparently, from the expression on Luke's face, nothing was making sense. So he held up his hand, and because we weren't immediately silent, he shouted, "Quiet!" That got our attention fast!

Luke pointed at Addy first, and said, "You were the first one I heard." Irritation was ringing in his voice as he stated, "Explain what happened."

Addy replied nervously, "Well, I woke up about a half-hour ago and tried to wake up Skye. She wouldn't wake up even though I tried really hard. Then, I spent more than a few minutes trying to wake up Leira. It was morning, and I was getting a little scared because neither of them would wake up. Just as I was about to call for you, Leira woke up and started to gripe at me."

Luke interjected, "Hold on. I want each of you to continue the story, but when I call out your name, I want that person to speak." Each of us understood, and we unraveled the moment's bit-by-bit. When we finished, Skye and Addy had their own questions about the symbols. Luke explained to them what we had found the previous night, but he didn't reveal that there was a mystery to solve. Addy was relieved to know that Luke had heard the coyotes as well. He looked at Skye and said, "You were right about them being a good distance away and nothing to worry about." Addy and I noticed that Skye's face reddened.

Addy explained to Luke, "Skye only slept a few hours last night because she was afraid of the coyotes. That's why I couldn't wake her up." Glancing over at Skye with a smile, Addy recognized a look of pure anger and humiliation on Skye's face.

Skye immediately retorted, "I was NOT afraid—they were just noisy!"

Luke smoothed out the fray by saying, "Skye, they are extremely noisy. They've kept me awake several times—in fact, they kept me awake part of the night."

Skye blushed again, apparently heartened by his declaration. In the meantime, Addy looked at me in utter confusion but seeing the sign of warning in my eyes, she decided not to comment. With a grin on my face, I cheerfully asked, "Now that we've settled that, can we have breakfast? I'm starved!"

Addy whispered to me, "I still need to use the privacy sheet, remember? And, is there something I should know about that I don't?"

I replied softly, "Sorry, and yes, there is something I need to explain. Just let me go get the items we need." After retrieving them, I held up the privacy sheet and said to Luke and Skye, "We'll be back in a few minutes." Addy asked Skye, "Do you want to come?" Exasperated, I poked her in the ribs with my elbow. She looked at me crossly and was about to make a sharp comment, when I whispered, "Sshhhh."

She asked quietly but irritably, "What's the problem?"

I quickly whispered back, "I need to speak with you alone." Addy's face reddened as she replied, "Oh, sorry." Luckily, Skye indicated that she didn't need to go with us. It was obvious to me why; as I watched her help Luke release the food bag from the tree. As Addy and I headed off to do our business I told her, "Skye has a major crush on Luke, but under no circumstances are you to say a word unless she says something first. Do you promise?"

Addy, eyes widening in comprehension, replied, "I promise. Things make more sense now, the way she always wants to be near him and blushing any time he says something nice. But...?"

I questioned, "But what?"

Addy asked, "Isn't she going to be upset when we have to go home to Connecticut?"

I gave Addy a swift hug and said to her, "You're a good friend to ask that, Addy. Don't worry, we'll find a way to cheer her up. Remember, we start Jr. High next year! There will be plenty of boys our own age to think about."

Addy blushed and said indignantly, "Well, not for me—at least not yet!"

When we arrived back in camp, we helped Skye and Luke get breakfast ready, which consisted of dry cereal and bananas washed down with spring water. We wouldn't have any more meat until we got home the following evening.

After finishing our breakfast, cleaning up and stowing away our food and gear, Luke said, "Before we leave I want to take some pictures of those symbols we saw last night. Leira can I borrow your dad's camera? It's much better than mine."

I replied, "Sure, here it is." We walked to the first spot, and much to our surprise, it was gone! Luke asked if any of us had removed them and we all shook our heads. It was creepy. We hiked to the second corner of the perimeter, and there was no trace left of what we had seen there either.

Addy asked Luke, "What's going on? You're not trying to scare us, are you?"

Skye rose to his defense stating, "He'd never do that. That's something my brother Liam would do." Addy and I tried to keep from grinning. She definitely had a massive crush on Luke.

Luke took a deep breath and replied, "I would never do that to any of you. And Leira, your mom and my parents know that, or they would never have consented to this trip."

We apologized, feeling ashamed and followed Luke to the final two sights. We were surprised to see the arrangements were still there. But, they seemed slightly different to me. Luke and I glanced at each other, but I kept my mouth shut for the time being.

After he finished taking pictures, Luke reassured us not to worry. There was no doubt from the tone of his voice that he found them intriguing, but harmless. He said he would check them again at the end of the day.

We headed back to camp and got ready for our last day of adventure. We agreed on the walk back that we'd try not to worry about the signs. We were having a terrific time, and we didn't want to spoil our last day. The four of us stood there with our packs and bags ready to go, but everyone seemed too quiet. I tried to change the mood of our group by cheerfully asking Luke, "Well, where are we off to?"

Addy interjected, "I hope we're not going to have to walk as far today because my legs are still aching."

Luke replied with a grin, "We will be hiking farther, but it won't be as steep as yesterday, so we'll arrive at our destination more quickly." Addy groaned miserably. We grabbed our walking sticks and headed off. After leaving the camp, I said to Luke, "So, you didn't answer my question. Where are we headed and what's there?"

Luke replied, "Why don't you just enjoy the scenery and leave the answer as a surprise."

I said, "Oh, terrific! I think we've had more than our share of surprises already! At least give us some clue as to where we're headed."

Luke replied, "OK, but let me know if I'm boring you." He pointed out different types of flora (plant and flowers), stating which ones could be used for food or medicine. He described how the ancient Indian tribes lived within their surroundings—what they ate, how they dressed, hunted and survived in what seemed to be a barren wilderness. But, as a few hours quickly ticked by, I started to appreciate what life must have been like for them. The more he spoke, the more fascinated I was by these extremely resourceful, intelligent and definitely hardy people. Skye and Addy were both quiet during the hike, so I figured they were as intrigued as I was.

About eleven o'clock, we stopped for a short time, nibbled on some granola bars, and drank water from a nearby spring, refilling our canteens before leaving. All of us remained quiet and thoughtful. Then, we continued our journey with Luke adding information every now and again. He weaved a spell around us with his descriptions of life in ancient desert times. Luke spoke of the Apache, Hopi and Sinagua Indians, and how shamefully 'The White Man' destroyed their people. He told us about the ancient Sanskrit pictograph, which had been discovered in the area only twenty-five years ago. This Sanskrit was anywhere from three to six thousand years old. They previously had only been found in places like India and Tibet. There was deep admiration in every word he spoke, and if I remembered nothing else, I would remember that intense feeling he conveyed.

We hiked another two hours or so before Luke stopped. Glancing back at us, he said, "Leira, Addy, Skye—get ready for the surprise. It's right around that rocky boulder!"

Chapter 11

What's For Dinner?

MONTEZUMA CASTLE

I felt my blood surge through my veins as I cautiously crept around the boulder, not knowing what to expect. Looking at Skye and Addy, I sensed that they felt the same anxious anticipation.

We followed Luke around the edge of the boulder and stopped—staring—trying to figure out what the surprise was. All three of us glanced back and forth at one another in ignorance, trying to avoid Luke's gaze. I felt ridiculous that none of us understood. All I could see were some strange holes in the cliffs above us.

Luke pointed directly at them and said, "Those are ancient Indian cliff dwellings built over a thousand years ago. Several native tribes built them, including the Sinagua, the Anasazi and the Hohokam. The last tribe disappeared about five hundred years ago. Some archeologists think that happened because of too little rainfall, disease or war."

Peering at the tiny holes in the sheer cliff, I asked in disbelief, "How could they possibly get up there? I don't see how someone, except a small child could fit through those holes."

Skye, Addy and I looked intently at Luke, waiting for the answer.

He replied, "Well, I can't say exactly how they got up from the bottom or down from the top. But researchers, who are knowledgeable about several of these native cultures, say the size of the average person, in this region was much smaller than people today. Archeologists have found human bones that show the significant size difference. As far as climbing up or down to get into the caves; I believe from what I've read that most likely they used a system of ropes that could have easily been made from the plant life surrounding us."

Addy questioned, "You mean they were like Tarzans of the desert?" Skye and I laughed at that remark, but Luke answered seriously, "I suppose you could look at it like that. But as I said, I don't know for sure."

I asked Luke, "Can we have a closer look?"

He responded, "Sure—but I don't have any ropes. But, it's afternoon, so let's have our lunch first."

"Great..." Addy said with a grimace. "What are we having? More granola bars?"

Luke laughed cheerfully and replied, "No, we're having super-sealed, peanut butter and jelly tortillas. They'll melt in your mouth like 'butter'."

I smirked at his teasing sarcasm, but because we were quite ravenous, we didn't complain. We each ate two, and although they didn't actually melt in our mouths, they stopped our stomachs from rumbling. After lunch, we hiked about twenty minutes to the base of the cliff dwellings. We still couldn't believe how people could climb into them. The face of the cliff was sheer rock, punctuated with a hundred or so small openings.

Luke explained, "There is a series of connecting mazes throughout the caves. Archeologists and historians investigated them many years ago, but now they are under the protection of the national parks. No further study of the interiors is allowed due to their age and condition of ruin." Luke added wishfully, "I'd love to get up inside there and go through those mazes."

Addy responded, "You couldn't get me in there if you paid me! I can't imagine what sort of creatures inhabit them now."

Skye laughed and replied, "Well, I don't think anyone except Leira is small enough to fit through THOSE holes!"

I never knew whether to be happy or mad about being what my mom termed 'petite'. Addy contributed, "Leira may be fit, but when she's wearing her hair up in a bun, it might get stuck. Or if she's wearing it down, the bats will get stuck!"

Even Luke chuckled at that statement. I was slightly irritated and embarrassed. My honey-brown hair had grown down past my waist, and most of the time, I kept it put up in some manner that I had created myself. I didn't appreciate Addy making fun of me.

Luke noticed my discomfort and said, "Leira, they're just teasing you because we're envious—that's all."

My anger vanished as I burst out in laughter, "Oh Luke! I never knew you wanted hair as long as mine." Addy, Skye and I began laughing hysterically as Luke realized his blunder, and for once, his face reddened in embarrassment.

Still giggling, I said, "Just teasing. Thanks for cheering me up."

Good natured, Luke replied, "OK, I get it." Just then, he glanced up at the sky. We followed his gaze. Ominous black clouds were moving quickly to cover the sun. Luke studied them a brief moment and said, "Those clouds could mean some serious storms and they are coming this way. Let's start hiking back now."

I replied, "Just let me take some pictures first." I began taking a dozen or so photos with my dad's super zoom digital camera when Luke interrupted and said, "Sorry Leira, we need to get going now. If we're lucky, these clouds will dissipate, but if not, we need to get moving at double speed."

Then Addy anxiously asked, "Are those the same cliffs we saw yesterday when the bear appeared?"

Luke replied, "Yes they are, but that was from a much greater distance."

Alarmed by Luke's response, Addy quickly stated, "Right! Let's get going now!"

Skye echoed Addy's reply with, "Yeah, we don't want to get caught in a storm."

I don't think any of us liked the idea of hunkering down in a storm or a double-speed pace, but remembering the bear, we quickly turned and started heading back. It had taken almost five hours to get here, not counting the breaks, and Luke said he wanted to make it back in two to three hours. That would get us back to camp between five and six o'clock. As we started off, Skye and I took one last glance at the cliff dwellings. Under the darkness of the storm clouds, I could have sworn I saw a light flicker in one of the caves. I looked at Skye and asked, "Did you see that?"

Skye hesitantly asked, "The light?"

"Yeah." I said. Skye immediately turned and began sprinting to catch up with the others. She shouted back at me, "Nope! I didn't see a thing—let's go!"

It took us slightly over three hours to reach camp. Luckily, the storm seemed to lessen a bit. The clouds still looked ominous, but didn't seem to be gaining on us. When we reached camp—out of breath and aching—Skye, Addy and I fell to the ground exhausted. Luke surveyed the sky and stated, "I think we could be in for a downpour, so let's get dinner ready and take care of everything in case it hits. It's very unusual to get a severe storm during the winter, but it's best to be prepared. I'll get the food down from the canvas. The three of you should go do any 'business' you might need to take care of and then come back to help me."

We grabbed the 'privacy sheet' and headed off to our usual secluded area. Afterwards, we filled up our canteens (along with Luke's) and headed back to camp. When we arrived, we stared in complete shock at what Luke was holding!

Fearfully, I asked, "What is that? What are you holding?" Neither Addy nor Skye could say anything.

Luke had an expression of deep concern and replied, "Apparently, our food has been discovered and eaten by a predator. Judging from the remains, it must have been particularly hungry." He was holding up the shredded remains of the canvas food bag. Littered beneath it were cans that had been bit and shredded apart.

Skye caught Addy as she nearly fainted. Cautiously, I asked, "What kind of animal do you think it was? Do you think it will come back?"

Luke replied tentatively, "With the amount of food it ate, I am fairly sure it won't come back. Most likely it was a mountain lion."

Skye trembled as Addy leaned against her once more. Luke continued, "As long as we keep a fire burning, there is little chance it will come back. It'll stay away from human scent. I'm positive we'll be fine tonight, don't worry."

He sounded confident, but I still felt uneasy. Considering the situation, I knew without a doubt that Luke would never put us in real peril. So, giving Luke a full show of support, I tried to lighten the conversation by asking teasingly, "Well, if 'whatever' ate all of our food, then what are we having for dinner?" Addy and Skye seemed to relax a bit at that question, and looked to Luke for an answer.

After some consideration, he replied, "Girls, I want you to relax in the tent. You can read, go over the day's events, play games, or whatever. I'm going to fix you a dinner that will delight your taste buds! Don't come out until I have everything ready."

Skye asked, "What if something awful happens and we need you?"

Luke replied, "I'll be within hearing distance at all times. The first thing I'm going to do is build a large fire."

Skye, Addy and I entered the tent. Tension filled the air as we sat down trying to calm our nerves. Addy inquired, "Well, what do you want to do while we're waiting?"

Skye asked, "Never mind that! What do you think he's going to make for dinner? I'm totally starved!"

I tried to dispel the tension by saying, "Whatever it is, I'm sure we'll like it! By the way, I wanted to ask both of you what you think of my cousin. I trust him completely, but he's my cousin, so I might be a little biased."

Addy, who immediately caught on to my train of thought (about Skye and Luke) said, "I think he's brilliant, Leira! We couldn't have had an adventure like this with anyone else. What do you think, Skye?"

Skye blushed as she thought over a proper response. Finally, she said, "Well, he's very knowledgeable and…"

Addy prompted, "And what?"

After considering for a minute or so, Skye said, "He's also very brave and—um—comforting." Addy and I gazed at her in anticipation. She added, "Every time I start to get worried, I feel like nothing bad will happen because he's with us." Then, looking at our expressions, she asked, "What's that look for? You guys are making me feel weird."

I responded tactfully, "It's nothing. I'm sure we all feel the same way, or we would have gone home a day or two ago. By the way, even though he's my cousin, I think he's fantastic and not bad looking. What do you think?"

Addy replied laughing, "I agree he's cute, but he's too old for me. Besides, my parents say they won't even let me think about boys for another few years!" Turning her attention to Skye, Addy asked, "What do you think of Luke? Would you want to go on a date with him?"

Skye's face drained to pale white. She replied stuttering, "What kind of question is THAT?"

I said quickly, "Look, Addy and I both admitted he's cute, and you told us he's brave and comforting, so can't you be honest about whether you like him?"

Skye replied, "Well, of course I like him, but I think both of you are saying I feel more than that."

Both Addy and I looked at her expectantly, and I said, "Skye, we're all best friends. We promise never to say a word to anyone if you like Luke more than a friend does. But, it would be nice if you trusted Addy and I enough to confide in us."

Obviously embarrassed, Skye replied, "OK, so what if I do like him? I know I'm only twelve, and he's eighteen. So just, let me enjoy this time. And you'd better keep your promise!" Staring at us intently, she added, "If either one of you say one word, I'll never speak to you again. Besides, maybe we can come back again when we're older, who knows? Now, can we drop the subject?"

Addy replied, "No problem. I'm just happy you've finally confided in us. How long has Luke been gone anyway?"

I glanced at my watch and said, "He's been gone a little over a half hour and I don't smell anything cooking. Why don't we play 'hangman' while we're waiting?" After playing for about forty-five minutes, we heard noises outside. All three of us looked up and listened breathlessly. I crept to the front zippered opening and asked in a quiet voice, "Luke—is that you?"

Last Night—Will we be flooded out?

A faint shadow crossed our tent. We breathed a huge sigh of relief when Luke responded, "It's just me, but don't come out until I have dinner ready. It'll take about a half hour."

I answered loudly, "Well hurry up! We are starving! It's almost seven-thirty."

Luke replied, slightly agitated, "Considering there's a heck of a storm boiling up, I'm going as quickly as I can."

"What storm?" I asked. I poked my head through the tent opening and while eyeing the sky, I said, "We can help you, and watch the storm coming." Addy elbowed me in the ribs at that statement. I looked at her sharply as she whispered, "Not ALL of us wants to see it!"

Luke replied sternly, "DON'T come out until I say so. You'll get a good look at those thunderheads soon enough. Now let me get busy with dinner."

Soon, the aroma of whatever he was cooking over the open fire filled our senses, and all of our tummies grumbled in response. I said, "I don't know what we're having, but, if it tastes half as good as it smells, it'll be delicious." Addy and Skye nodded in agreement. We continued playing cards until Luke told us that dinner was ready.

When Luke called for us to come out, we quickly emerged from the tent. At the exact moment we stepped outside, we saw a jagged bolt of lightning in the distance. Ominous rumblings of thunder soon followed it. Forgetting my famished stomach, I asked Luke, "Are you sure it's safe to be out here?"

Luke replied, "It's only for a short while. I've prepared three plates of food for you to take inside the tent. I'm going to set up rain fly's over your tent and my sleeping area while you're eating." After he handed us our plates, Addy and I re-entered the tent. But, before Skye stepped through the opening, she turned and asked Luke with concern, "What about your dinner? When are you going to eat?"

Luke replied smiling, "Don't worry about me. I've fixed a plate for myself. Skye, if you don't mind, could you put it inside the tent for me? There's a pan covering it to keep it warm. Also, here's a small bowl of dipping sauce—use it with any of the foods you'd like. It's good with all three."

I asked, "What exactly is it that we're eating?" Just then, another flash of lightening lit up the sky! An ear-splitting crack of thunder quickly followed. Addy screamed, I shuddered, and Skye almost dropped the bowl of sauce!

Luke shouted after the thunder lessened, "I'll tell you when I'm finished, so just eat and enjoy." With that, he zipped us in.

After sitting down on a comfortable spot, Addy said, "I'm not sure what these three things are, but they sure smell terrific. Let's eat!" With her fork, she pierced a circular-shaped item about the size of a small pancake, which Luke had apparently grilled. Skye and I watched as she sniffed it, and then took a little bite. A smile emerged on her face as she chewed it.

She took a much larger bite, and with her mouth still full she mumbled, "It's heavenly."

Skye and I stabbed the circular shaped things, and as we began stuffing our mouths, smiles broke out on our faces. Between bites, Skye dipped her finger in the sauce and licked it. Her eyes lit up in delight as she told us to try it. We did, and we were even more impressed with Luke's cooking.

After Addy had finished her pancake things, she stabbed her fork into a thick chunk of something white that the fire had blackened. She smelled it first and said, "Ooh, its smells like chicken." She was just about to take a bite when the tent lit up from another bolt of lightning. A loud rumble of thunder followed, and shortly after, we heard the sound of gently falling rain. As Addy shrugged and started chewing her second course of food, I shouted out, "Luke, are you almost done?"

He yelled back, "Yes, I'll be done in a few minutes—just eat up and don't touch mine!"

Skye said smugly, "I told you he's brave." At that point, Skye and I scooped up the large pieces of 'whatever' and started eating. After a few moments, we finished our pieces, and I replied somewhat tentatively, "I don't know what this is, but it doesn't taste anything like chicken."

Skye agreed, but said, "Let's put some sauce on it. That should make it taste even better." Because we were so hungry, we finished whatever it was drenched in the sweet but slightly spicy sauce. We hardly noticed that the rain was coming down more heavily.

The last thing on our plates looked like some type of rolled flat bread. After tasting it, I informed my friends that it was like a tortilla wrapped around some kind sugary nuts. Enthusiastically, we polished off the remainder of the food on our plates. Unfortunately, for Luke, we didn't leave any sauce.

Just as we were finishing up, Luke shouted to me to let him into the tent. I unzipped it, and he entered through a driving sheet of rain.

Heavily drenched with his clothes plastered on him, Luke turned and effortlessly zipped the tent back up in a flash. Turning around and moving quickly to the side away from our sleeping bag area, he looked a bit chagrined as he stated, "I guess I was wrong about storms in the winter."

Skye, taking in the sight of him, responded with a smile, "Well, no one can be right all the time, but we did enjoy our dinner."

Luke had a small, partially dry towel stuffed under his shirt and dried himself off as good as he could. He was still wet, but at least he wasn't dripping. He plunked down on the ground and said, "We're OK for now, but I'm starved."

Skye handed him his lukewarm plate and he began eating with gusto. He didn't seem to mind that we had used up all of his special sauce. We remained silent as the rain pelted down. When he finished, Luke looked at us and asked, "So did everyone enjoy your desert delight dinner?"

The lightning and thunder were starting to taper off as I replied, "Well, those pancake-shaped things were fantastic, especially with the sauce, and the little tortilla things that had some kind of nuts in them were good, but this other stuff was sort of dry and had a strange flavor which I didn't like too much."

Skye added, "We dipped each piece in the sauce and ate every bit, though."

Addy then inquired, "So, what kind of plants or whatever did we eat?"

Luke replied, "The 'pancakes' are prickly pear cactus. I removed all of the spines and cut them in half using the liquid inside to help make the sauce. Then I grilled them. While they were cooking, I added other seasonings from home to the sauce, and boiled that over the fire until it thickened."

I interjected, "Those were really fantastic Luke. But what was the other stuff we ate?"

Luke replied, "I made you a real delicacy, especially because of how hard it was to find and kill."

All three of us looked a bit worried as I inquired, "Killed? We thought it smelled a bit like chicken, but it didn't taste like it at all. Was it some type of bird?"

Anxiously awaiting his answer, he replied, "No, it was rattlesnake and I had a heck of a time finding two and killing them."

We stared at him in shock, and I gasped, "You're telling me I just ate rattlesnake?" Addy went pale and said, "I think I'm going to be sick."

Addy gulped, trying to keep her meal down, then, I looked at Skye who was too quiet. Nudging her, I asked, "Skye, aren't you going to say anything?"

Skye stammered, "Luke, I can't believe you did something so dangerous just to feed us. You are so awesome!" As Skye's face reddened, Luke perceived her fondness for him. He quickly said, "No problem. By the way, the 'tortilla-nut things' as you called them were mesquite tortillas filled with mesquite pads (or nuts) if you prefer. I added a bit of sugar to make them sweeter."

Trying to be cheerful, I responded, "Yes. They were terrific!"

Luke had a thoughtful expression on his face and finally looked up realizing what he had forgotten, and stated. "Oh yeah, I forgot to give you your dessert." Out of his soaked pack, which he had brought in with him, he produced four chocolate chip granola bars. He said, "I'm assuming the rain didn't get through the wrappers." He handed one to each of us and began consuming his. After finishing our bars, I glanced up and asked, "Weren't these supposed to be part of our breakfast or snacks for tomorrow?"

He replied, "Yes, they were, but don't worry about that now. The storm has almost passed. We should try to get a decent night's sleep before our return home tomorrow. Therefore, do any of you need to 'take care of business' while I inspect your tent?"

We silently nodded our heads and left the tent. When we arrived back, he zipped us in and said, "Breakfast will probably be more prickly pear cactus—is that all right with you?"

I replied, "That would be great, especially if you can make some more sauce. Can you?"

Laughing, Luke replied, "Yes, and you can help me. Have a good night."

Shortly after midnight, an unexpected bright flash awakened Skye, Addy and me. An enormous clap of thunder immediately followed it. I tried to sit up quickly, but my sleeping bag confined me as the zipper caught on another snag. A second bolt of lightning quickly lit our tent brighter than daylight, and I caught a glimpse of Skye and Addy trying unsuccessfully to sit up too. Then came an ear-shattering crack of thunder. All three of us rolled our bags towards one another for protection. Simultaneously, we screamed, "LUKE!"

Fear pulsed through me as I realized the tent was zipped open and a dark figure was hunched in the doorway! As the thunder retreated, I heard the sound of the tent zipper closing. I thought to myself, "This has to be a nightmare." It was then that I heard Luke shouting to us, "It's only me, don't be afraid!"

Another flash lit the tent, and the pounding rain deafened our hearing as we tried to talk. Shortly, thereafter came another terrifying flash of light, followed just as quickly by a trembling blast of thunder. Luke turned on a flashlight and saw that Skye, Addy and I were in a complete panic. Trying to raise his voice above the sporadic lightning and thunder, Luke said to us that we were safe, and the storm would end shortly. That didn't comfort me when the tent started to sway violently. The pelting rain seemed like bullets raining down on us.

I screamed, "Luke! What's happening?"

Luke yelled back, "Just huddle down together! This will be over soon."

I heard Addy screeching, "Yeah, right! I thought we were done with…" More lightning and cracks of thunder drowned out the rest of her sentence. The three of us huddled together, and I felt Luke sit down beside me. He was shaking, and it made me realize how cold it had gotten. When there was a short break after the thunder I asked Luke, "Are you all, right? You're shivering."

Before the next flash and rumble, he managed to say, "I'm all right, just cold. This storm will…." At that instant, his reply was drowned out again. I waited for another break. Thankfully, the storm seemed to be moving away. I asked, "Is there anything I can do?"

Luke replied, "No. You're doing great, and we'll be fine. The storm is almost gone." I could hear Skye or Addy crying softly. As each minute ticked by, the storm lessened. When I felt reasonably composed, I asked Luke if the worst of it had passed.

Luke, who was still shaking slightly, sat up straight and said, "That's the end of it. Everything will be alright now."

Addy sat up shrieking, "YOU SAID THERE WOULDN'T BE ANY RAIN—NEVER MIND A LIGHTENING AND HAIL STORM!" She began to cry. Luke tried to soothe her saying, "I'm so sorry Addy. This type of occurrence has never happened in my life, although I've heard of it. I don't know if you'll believe it, or not, but the last time this happened was about thirty years ago. I'm so sorry."

The storm was definitely moving away as Skye said, "I believe you Luke, but I'm happy we're going back to your mom's tomorrow. It's been an adventure I'll never forget."

As Addy tried to stifle her tears, I asked Luke, "Why are you shivering so badly?"

Luke replied, "I'd been awake for about an hour or so since I realized the storm was coming. The temperature dropped dramatically, and my new 'waterproof' sleeping bag has proven useless. The company that sold it to me is in for a big shock."

I said, "Well, the tent has held up great! Do you have any dry clothes? We have an extra blanket here for you to curl up with."

Luke replied, "Thanks, cous….I'll be back in a few minutes." The rain was only lightly pattering down on the tent as he crawled back in, with dry clothes. He thankfully accepted our extra blanket, and some used clothes to rest his head on. Within minutes, he was sound asleep and so were Skye and Addy. The last thing I heard while falling asleep was the soft snores of my cousin and friend's….and in the distance, one lone howl of a coyote—or maybe, I was dreaming.

Chapter 13

Packing Up

A few hours had drifted by when I awoke. Luke had left the tent. I felt damp and cold, even though I was snuggled deep into my sleeping bag. Unzipping it, I shivered and put on my sweatshirt, rubbing my hands together to warm them. My movements awakened Skye because she sleepily asked, "Leira, what are you doing?"

Whispering, I replied, "Luke's left and I'm going looking for him. Do you want to come with me?"

Skye answered, "Yeah, but what about Addy? She'll be terrified if she wakes up and nobody's around."

I responded a bit irritably, "Well, wake her up then. I'll be right outside the tent." I exited the tent and gasped! All that remained of our large campfire was scattered everywhere. There were even small trees and branches lying nearby. Luke's rain fly was gone. I looked anxiously around but I didn't see him. The ground glistened from the remnants of the hail, and the sky was tinted a vibrant, iridescent orange-red. Unfortunately, the beauty of my surroundings didn't comfort me. I desperately called out "LUKE, LUKE, where are you?"

Addy and Skye stepped out of the tent, and I could sense they felt the same way I did, by the expressions on their faces. Just as Skye started to ask me a question, I heard Luke yelling, "It's OK Leira! I'll be there in a minute."

Breathing a sigh of relief, I turned to Skye and Addy and said, "I don't know how to describe how I feel. Part of me is extremely scared, but another part of me feels relieved that we're alright." Luke emerged from around the corner with a couple of plates, a pan and a few utensils. Looking at them closely, I could see how banged up they were. I asked in astonishment, "Is that all that's left of our cooking supplies?"

Luke nodded his head and said down-heartedly, "The storm ripped through the camp pretty hard. But if the three of you look up at the sky you'll see something rare." He waited a moment, and then asked, "Do you see the double rainbow? That only happens after a winter storm like the one we had early this morning. I've never seen this phenomenon before, but I've read about it."

Addy softly stated in wonderment, "It's simply beautiful."

Skye added, "Especially, with the way the water glistens on everything. It's kind of like seeing the trees back home after an ice storm."

Shivering, I asked Luke, "It's so cold, aren't you going to light a fire and cook us some breakfast?"

"Leira." Luke responded patiently, "There's not a dry piece of anything to burn unless you want to burn your dirty clothes. Do you understand? Everything I packed and covered got saturated." Holding up his backpack, he said, "Look, the metal rods have been severely bent from being knocked against the rocks during the storm. I won't even be able to strap it on. Luckily, yours were inside the tent. I lost both rain flys, although I did find one of them, but it was shredded badly." Luke spread the mangled sheet on the ground for us to sit on.

Anxiously, Addy asked, "So, what are we going to eat for breakfast?"

Luke replied, holding out the battered pan, "I've collected enough cactus for us, but I won't be able to grill them or make any sauce. It would be a tremendous help if the three of you would help me take the spines off."

As the three of us looked at him fearfully, he replied, "Don't worry, I haven't stuck myself yet." That statement didn't particularly make me feel better. Luke continued, "I'll show you how it's done and while you're doing that, I'll start packing up camp. One thing is for sure, we won't have half as much to carry back."

After Luke showed us how to take out the spines, we sat down and began our work. Shortly thereafter, I realized I wasn't shivering anymore. In fact, the warmth of the morning sun felt fantastic. My spirits were rising with the increase of temperature. By the time we finished, we noticed Luke had packed up our belongings and fastened our sleeping bags on top of the backpacks. They definitely looked much lighter than when we had hiked down.

Luke came over and said, "While I cut these cacti up, why don't the three of you go take care of business. Unfortunately, we lost the privacy sheet and paper, so why don't you go behind the tent before I pack it up?"

We must have looked extremely embarrassed, so Luke promised to stay put, and we grudgingly did as he asked. Once we were out of earshot, Addy said, "I'm sure I'll look back on this someday and laugh about it, but right now I can't wait to get back to our hotel, have a relaxing bath and a huge steak dinner."

I giggled and said, "Ditto for me! It won't be long before we're back. My mom wanted me to have an incredible adventure, and we've certainly had something like that!"

Skye raised her brow and replied skeptically, "You call this 'wonderful'?"

I replied, "Well, maybe not wonderful, but it sure was exciting." We arrived back just as Luke was cutting up the final piece of cactus. We noticed he was draining its juice into a battered cup.

Luke looked up and said, "You guys did a terrific job pulling out the spines."

Addy asked, "Why are you pouring the liquid into the cup?"

Luke replied, "This was the base of the sauce I made last night and although I can't cook it, it's still very sweet to drink. I thought you would like something other than spring water for a change."

We all sat down on the shredded, but dry rain fly and started chewing on the cactus pads. They weren't half as good as the ones we had eaten the previous night, but they were filling. We each took small sips of the cactus juice and agreed it was good. When we finished, Luke said, "I have a tiny surprise: I found the last two granola bars, so after we've finished packing everything and are ready to leave we can split them for a treat. Also, I have a few more snacks back at the jeep so we can munch on them until we get into town and pick up more food for the remainder of the drive home."

I felt comforted by that statement because I knew we would be starving by the time we made it back to the jeep. It took about an hour to clear out camp. By then, we were warm enough to take off our sweatshirts. Because we'd lost our canvas bags to the mountain lion, Luke was undecided what to do with our trash. It was a big taboo to leave it in the desert.

Addy suggested, "Why don't we put the trash and what's left of our cooking supplies in your backpack, Luke? The empty cans shouldn't weigh that much."

Luke looked at Addy and replied, "That's a terrific idea. Thanks, Addy!"

I noticed Skye had a sour look on her face. She probably wished she had come up with the idea. I whispered in her ear, "Don't feel bad Skye, you know you've helped Luke more than Addy, or I have."

Skye glanced at me and replied, "Thanks, Leira."

After that, we picked up everything we could find that Luke considered trash and put it into his backpack. When we finished, Luke tested its weight and said, "This won't be any problem for me to carry."

Then I inquired, "What about the tent? You had it fastened to your backpack, so how are you going to carry that now?"

Before Luke could respond, Skye said quickly, "I can carry the tent. You said it only weighs fourteen pounds. I can handle that."

Luke responded, "Skye, you're a sweetheart for offering (she blushed at that remark), but it might be a bit too much for the hike back."

I saw Skye was upset, so I said, "Well, my pack and Addy's aren't half as heavy as they were on the way down so why don't we transfer some of Skye's stuff into ours?"

Luke considered my suggestion, and then replied, "I think I'm OK with that. Skye, is that alright with you?"

Skye immediately lit up with a brilliant smile and said, "Absolutely!" We rearranged the contents of our packs and tried them on. Luke checked each one and said, "I think this is manageable. Remember, we need to have our hands free, one for our walking sticks and one to hold on to each other, if needed." With that, Luke walked over to the tent, had it collapsed, and ready to fit on Skye's backpack within a minute. After he attached it, he fitted the pack onto Skye, inquiring, "How does that feel?"

Skye confidently replied, "It's fine. It's still lighter than the one I carried down here."

Luke said, "OK then campers, take off your packs and let's go fill our canteens and make one last walk around the perimeter to see if there's anything else we've left behind."

Propping our four backpacks on the shredded rain fly (which we would also stuff into Luke's pack), we headed to the spring. As we were filling our canteens, Luke gazed over to where we had seen the first of the strange configurations. To his astonishment (and ours), there was another arrangement of sticks and stones. The four of us slowly walked over and studied it. This new configuration had more unique engravings on the stones and designs scored into the ground around them. Luke said softly, "Leira, you and Addy go back to your pack and get the camera. Skye, you stay here with me." As we started to walk away, Luke added, "Make it snappy, but don't forget to keep your eyes peeled for snakes or scorpions."

Addy whispered to me, "Oh terrific! My skin is already crawling from the new symbols. Then, he has to remind me of snakes and scorpions!"

I whispered back, "Be quiet! He's just watching out for us." We arrived back quickly. I handed my camera to Luke, and he took four pictures, each from a different angle. When he finished, I asked, "Who do you think put them there?"

"Yeah." Demanded Addy, "They certainly couldn't have been there before the storm ended or they would have been gone by now."

Skye said tensely, "Then someone arranged them after the storm."

Addy, her eyes widening, gasped, "Oh my gosh! What if whoever put these here watched us go to the bathroom behind the tent this morning?"

Skye and I stifled the laughter boiling up in us as I tried to reply calmly, "Addy, that's the last thing we need to worry about. Luke, can you figure out what it means?"

Luke answered slowly, "No, not without my computer. I haven't seen anyone, and there are no footprints. That probably means whoever placed these here are knowledgeable about Indian customs and know how to keep themselves 'invisible'."

I asked hesitantly, "What do you mean by 'invisible'?"

Luke responded, "Native American Indians were masters of traveling on foot without leaving any trace. They could also maintain complete silence in their travels. Whoever placed this here has the same capability. But, I still don't believe that whoever it was means us any harm. Let's go check the other three points of the camp while we make a final check of any scattered items that might have been blown away."

As Luke started to leave, Addy confronted him, "If you already surveyed the area, why didn't you find that 'thing' before?"

Luke looked her straight in the eye and said, "Because, they weren't there before. No more questions—just look for debris left from our encampment."

Alarmed by Luke's pronouncement, each of us was speechless. As we continued to search the area, we kept close to Luke. Nearing the second corner of our campsite, Addy screamed, turned around and ran back a short distance. Skye and I stopped dead in our tracks. Luke yelled to Addy, "What is it?"

Addy tearfully replied, "A scorpion!"

Skye and I took a few steps backwards as Luke began searching the area. Finally, Luke acknowledged, "It is a scorpion. But Addy, you need to get a grip on yourself. You nearly gave Skye and Leira a heart attack. I want the three of you to come here—NOW."

Cautiously, we approached Luke. He pointed towards the scorpion with his walking stick and said, "That—is a scorpion. Get a good look at it, so you'll know in the future the difference between a wind spider and a real scorpion."

Each of us kept our distance, but was still close enough to scrutinize it. Then, Luke said, "Now, let's get going. It's almost ten-thirty."

We followed Luke particularly closely. Shortly thereafter, we came upon another arrangement of sticks and painted stones. Nervous, but intrigued, I handed Luke my camera so he could take more pictures. None of us asked questions this time. We just wanted to get going.

Upon reaching the next section of the encampment, we came upon a third set of symbols. This time there were no sticks, just stones with inscriptions on them. As Luke took more pictures, I noticed one of our forks lying on the ground and picked it up. I showed Luke the fork. He took it and placed it in my backpack, saying, "Good job Leira."

After several more minutes of searching, we came to the final corner of our encampment area. There we found an arrangement of sticks, with one of our spoons protruding from the center. Something about the way the spoon was placed frightened me, so apprehensively, I asked Luke, "Do we remove it?"

Luke hesitated before saying, "Yes. It's the law of the desert not to leave anything behind that disturbs the natural environment." With that, he dislodged the spoon and was about to place it in my pack when I backed away. Skye and Addy did the same.

Luke said, "Leira, let me put this in your pack for now. I'll transfer it to mine when we reach base camp."

I looked at him in dread and replied, "I'm really sorry, but for some reason I don't want to touch it or carry it."

Skye stepped forward and said, "Give it to me. I'll carry it."

Luke smiled and said, "Thank you, Skye." He placed the spoon in Skye's backpack. Then he took a few more pictures and said, "Do any of you want your half of the granola bars before we head out?"

Apparently, none of us were hungry, so I said, "Let's just get going. When we're away from here, maybe food will seem more important."

Luke replied, "Right then! Let's be off."

Chapter 14

An Accident

As we began our trek across the desert floor towards the first area of ascent, I quickly became aware of how slippery the ground was in certain areas. Luke stopped after ten minutes or so and said, "Hold up for a bit." Stopping, he explained, "This ground is still extremely wet in spots, which means we'll have to take our time hiking back to the jeep. I don't think there should be any problem, but try and stick to the dryer areas or patches of scrub brush along the trail."

Addy sarcastically asked, "You mean you WANT us to step on the cholla cacti?"

Luke teasingly replied, "Of course. I'm dying to use my cholla comb on you." Taking a deep breath, he continued, "Seriously though, concentrate on your footing and let me know immediately if you have any trouble. Are there any questions?"

We shook our heads, and Luke said, "Good. Oh, and one more thing, give a hand to the person behind you if needed. We'll switch positions every ten or so minutes like we did on the way down. It will probably take about an hour to reach the next level. If you remember, it's an easy walk for about a half hour when we get there. Is everyone ready?"

Skye replied, "I'm ready Luke—let's go!"

Luke smiled at Skye, and her face reddened as we began climbing.

When we reached the base and looked upward, it seemed much more menacing than it had on the way down. I'm sure Skye was recalling her encounter with the prickly pear cactus. We put our walking sticks to good use after the first hundred feet or so. Not only did they help us maintain our balance and support but also, by prodding the ground with them, we could tell if the ground was firm, rocky or muddy. Skye took Addy's hand when she needed help, just as Addy took mine and I took Luke's. I imagined that Skye was anticipating her turn to hold his hand. I grinned to myself as we continued up the steepest part of our ascent into the canyon from the desert floor.

When we had reached a non-treacherous section, we switched places, with Luke still in front, then Addy, Skye and I trailing behind him.

Luke stopped at various places in order to choose the most solid ground for the following several steps. He explained what he was doing and told us to do our best to walk exactly where he did.

We had just made our way to another changing point. Addy let go of Luke's hand to let Skye and I pass, but she didn't grab my hand when we started moving again. Skye, (apparently in seventh heaven) holding Luke's hand, didn't notice I had stopped until she felt the tug. I turned quickly and noticed the look of terror on Addy's face just as she screamed. I called to the others, "Stop! Something's wrong with Addy!"

Luke whirled about, steadied Skye, and quickly reached Addy's side. Luke asked hurriedly, "Addy, what's wrong? Are you hurt?"

Addy, trembling, could only point her finger at her foot. There, on the top of her sneaker sat a huge tarantula that actually covered almost half of the shoe! Luke, in a calming voice said, "Addy, you're all right. I'm going to take hold of your arm, and then I'm going to bend down and take this fellow away from you."

At that instant, Skye burst out, "NO! You'll be bit!"

Luke's eyes blazed at Skye in annoyance. Keeping his voice calm, he continued, "There will be no problem if everyone stays still and quiet." Before bending down, Luke glanced up at Addy to make sure she was still and much to his relief found Addy still as a statue. He bent down and with the end of his walking stick prodded the ugly, furry fellow off her, towards a safer spot. Standing up, he rubbed Addy's shoulders as if trying to warm her and asked, "Are you OK? Do you want to stand here for a few minutes, or get going?"

Addy looked up at him with tears in her eyes and hoarsely replied, "Let's get going—now."

Luke smiled and said, "You're a real trooper. Come on, we're over half way to the level plain."

Even though Luke had taken hold of Skye's hand again, I noticed her trembling in embarrassment from her earlier outburst. I gave her hand several hug-squeezes, but she didn't acknowledge them. Addy stopped abruptly after a few steps. All of us felt a little tug, and Luke stopped and turned around. He noticed Addy looking around fearfully. He walked down the few steps then asked, "Addy, what's wrong? Are you still worried about the spider?"

Addy's dark blue eyes looked up at Luke, as she replied irritably, "No! I've lost my walking stick. I must have dropped it when I saw the tarantula."

After the four of us scoured a small area looking for it without success, Luke finally surmised, "It must have rolled over that small drop off to our right. There's no use in trying to find it now."

Addy anxiously complained, "I can't go on without my stick! I won't be able to make the climb."

With tears welling up in her eyes again, Luke replied, "That's no problem." And with that, he took his own walking stick, broke off a little more than a foot and handed the whole thing to Addy.

Addy gaped at the shortened stick and stuttered, "You can't do that! Now you don't have one!"

Luke casually replied, "I'm fine without one. Now let's get going before we have to spend the night here."

After noticing the smile lurking in his eyes, we continued our climb.

Luke, who had recognized Skye's crush on him early into the camping trip, squeezed her hand and said quietly, "Don't feel bad Skye, I appreciate your concern. I wish all people were so caring."

Skye looked downwards and muttered, "Thanks, Luke."

He replied, "No problem."

It took more than an hour to finish the second portion of our upward climb before we finally reached the plateau. It was almost noon, and we were exhausted, but we carefully checked out the ground around us. After assuring one another that there wasn't anything dangerous nearby, we collapsed onto the desert floor. Gulping down the refreshing spring water, I suddenly remembered the granola bars Luke had promised us. I asked him, "Hey, where are those snacks you promised us? You didn't eat them, did you?"

Luke smiled and replied, "No, I didn't eat them, Leira. I was just saving them for when you were hungry enough to ask." He reached into the front of his backpack and pulled out the two bars. Breaking them in half, he handed pieces to each of us.

We grabbed our pieces and ate them, relishing each bite with small sips of fresh water in between. After a silent ten-minute rest, Luke said, "Let's get going. We have an easy half-hour walk until the next climb." We groaned, but knew that for a while; at least, it would be relatively easy going with the exception of watching out for snakes and stuff.

We refilled our canteens at a near-by spring and kept a steady pace until we came to the next part of the hike. It wasn't quite as steep as the previous ascent, but it had scary twisting pathways. Luke stopped and stated, "It's about twelve-forty-five now, so let's take a breather while I go cut some cactus to munch on; sorry for such a pitiful lunch. I could try to kill a snake or two and light a fire. I should be able to find some dry brush and twigs somewhere. What do you think?"

I replied, "Prickly pear cactus is fine for me. I think I'll skip the snake. I'd rather keep moving so we can get back to the jeep as soon as possible, where you said you had 'real' snacks!"

Skye and Addy echoed their agreement, so Luke headed off. Addy said, "I'd rather keep going too. The quicker we're back, the sooner we'll have real food."

I responded, "It'll go faster if we help Luke take the spines out." After several minutes, Luke arrived back with four large cactus pads. We each took the spines out of our own 'lunch'. Then Luke carefully cut them in half so the liquid wouldn't escape. We sipped the heavenly nectar—at least which was what it seemed like after drinking just water for almost four days. After we finished eating, I said, "Well, I'm not full, but I'm not starving either."

Skye added, "Same here, Leira." Turning to Luke, she asked, "Can we get going now?"

Luke replied, "Let's wash our hands in the spring, and then we'll be on our way." I glanced at my watch and saw it was after one o'clock. It had taken longer to fix and eat our lunch than I'd expected.

As we began the next climb, I realized this section of the path was wetter in places than the previous trail. I asked Luke, whose hand I was now holding, "Why is this section muddier than the first parts of our journey?"

Luke replied, "Well, the first hike up was much steeper and had more rock. So although it was very moist, most of the rain ran off it and the morning sun helped dry it a little. This part of the hike, not being as steep, has many places where the water has settled, instead of drained. The sun is blocked from many areas because of the way the path twists and turns. There's one more factor to consider; as this trail turns, the overhanging cacti, bushes and small trees block sunlight. That keeps the ground from drying as quickly. Everything should be dry by nightfall, but right now, it's tricky going. Do you have any other questions?"

Shaking our heads, we continued the hike upwards. We were about three-quarters of the way to the top when Luke stopped. The pathway had become extremely muddy, and we were nearing the spot with the sheer drop-off we had seen on the way down. Nervously, we waited for Luke to instruct us. He set his backpack down and asked Skye for her walking stick. Then he told us, "Stay here, I'll just be a minute or two."

He disappeared around the steep curve. He reappeared, after seeming to be gone forever, and said, "I'm sorry I've taken a while, but we're at the thin part of the trail that drops away quickly. The pathway is slippery, and the rain has washed a portion of it away, so it's much narrower now. We'll have to take extra precautions while climbing through this part. Here's what we need to do. I don't want anyone burdened by their backpacks during this part of the climb, so I'm going to take each of your packs up one at a time and place them safely above the drop-off. We'll redistribute the weight because I don't want the tent hanging off Skye's pack. We'll shift all of the things in Leira's pack to Addy's and yours, Skye. Then I'll put the tent inside Leira's. All I want you to have are your walking sticks. After I finish moving the packs, I'll lead you one at a time to where I've placed the packs. Is everyone clear?"

I asked shakily, "What about your pack? You're carrying it, so won't you be putting yourself in a risky position?"

Addy and Skye looked panic stricken at my question, but Luke calmly replied, "I'm going to take my pack up a little ways and then I'm going to use my best throwing arm to send it uphill. If for some reason my aim is bad, I'll worry about that later. I need a new pack anyway, but I don't want to leave 'trash' here. Sort out your things, I'll be right back." Carrying Skye's walking stick, he headed back up the twisting path, swinging his arm like a football quarterback getting ready to throw a touchdown. Just prior to going out of sight, he turned his head towards me, winked, and then with his next step vanished around the corner.

We just finished redistributing the weight, when Luke returned and took my pack with the tent in it then headed back up the embankment. I was so nervous, I almost forgot to ask, "How was your aim?"

He glanced back, smiling and replied, "Great! I should become a quarterback or a baseball pitcher." Addy responded with a grimace and asked, "Huh? What did you say?"

Luke replied, "Never mind, I'll explain later." He returned more quickly this time and took Addy's pack, which had all of our personal items and what were left of our cooking and eating utensils. As Luke hoisted it up on his shoulders, it clanked atrociously. He looked back at us and said, "Maybe we'll redistribute again after we've reached the plateau. The noise of this thing will scare every desert creature away."

Addy cheerfully replied, "Perfect! Let's leave it exactly the way it is!"

Luke smiled as he headed upwards once more. When he returned, he said, "Now, I'm going to take you up, Leira."

I quickly replied, "What, why me? You haven't taken Skye's pack up yet."

Luke said, "There are three packs up there, and I want to get you and Addy up there quickly to keep an eye on them."

Addy, alarmed asked, "Keep an eye on them? Are they going to walk away or something?"

Luke chuckled and then replied, "No, but no questions until I've got you and Leira up there with them."

Grabbing Luke's hand tightly with my own and my walking stick with the other, I headed toward the drop-off. I whispered to Luke hoping no one else could hear, "Don't let me fall." His eyes twinkled in return as he whispered back, "Don't worry, I wouldn't let anything happen to my favorite cousin."

It was utterly terrifying! I tried not to glance over the edge, but I couldn't help myself. Incredibly, before I began shaking from what I saw, I was over the slippery, narrow mud and standing next to the three backpacks.

Luke said, "Keep your stick handy. If anything moves towards them, sweep it away with your stick." It then dawned on me that Luke wanted us here to keep critters away from the packs. As he started back for Addy, I blurted out, "Well hurry up, I don't want to be here alone." My face reddened as I realized how frightened I sounded, so I quickly added, "Well, don't hurry too fast, just be careful." Luke nodded understandingly.

Addy was by my side before I knew it, shaking uncontrollably. I asked, "Did you look down?" Addy just nodded her head. But the terror in her eyes spoke more loudly than words.

Luke left to bring up Skye, and after he was out of sight, trembling, I asked Addy, "What about a stick, he doesn't have a walking stick. That one is Skye's. Should I go after him?"

Addy grabbed my arm firmly and stated, "Leira—NO WAY! He knows what he's doing, and he'll come back for it if he needs it." Mulling over the image of the steep cliff, I decided she was right.

Luke finally reached Skye's side and shouldered her backpack. He said, "Come-on, take my hand and let's go."

Skye blushed, and asked quietly, "You won't let go if I stumble—will you?"

Luke looked straight into her vivid green eyes and said, "I promise never to let you go."

Skye's heart soared with delight upon that statement and with an enormous grin, they headed up the treacherous path. With Luke holding her hand tightly, they climbed one treacherous step at a time up towards the curve. Skye, whose feelings were still joyous, wasn't keeping her eyes on the ground but on Luke. Before she knew what was happening, the ground crumbled beneath her right foot, and she had lost her balance!

Suddenly, Addy and I heard an ear-shattering scream! It seemed to go on forever.

Chapter 15

A Cry for Help!

Both Addy and I were in shock as the screaming continued. Disregarding the backpacks, we quickly but carefully made our way down the embankment towards Luke and Skye. As we rounded the bend we stopped, horrified! Luke was lying on the ground with both hands wrapped around what appeared to be Skye's wrist. Apparently, he was trying to pull her up from the edge of the drop-off. But, there was nothing to dig into and, he was slowly beginning to slip forward in the mud.

Desperately, I shouted to Luke, "How can we help?" He hastily asked, "Do you have your sticks?"

Together, Addy and I responded instantly, "Yes!"

He tried to reassure Skye, calmly, but firmly saying, "Skye, stop screaming and struggling. I've got you! Everything will be all right—I won't let go. Now look at me!" Skye, tearfully and silently looked at Luke.

Luke replied, "Good, just keep your pretty green eyes fastened on mine."

Without looking back at us, he commanded, "Addy, Leira, do you see that tree over there to the left of my head? It's standing on solid ground."

I replied, "Yes."

Luke quickly continued, "Both of you hurry over to it and clasp each other's hands behind the tree, and hold on tightly. With your other hands, extend your sticks together as far as you can to Skye. Once Skye has a good grip, I'll tell you to start backing up. Hurry!"

Soothingly, Luke said to Skye, "When I tell you to, reach up with your other hand, firmly grab those sticks and we'll pull you up. Do not wiggle, just hold on tight! Understand?" Skye nodded.

In an instant, we had positioned ourselves as Luke had instructed, gripping our sticks tightly as we extended them towards Skye's other hand that had appeared over the edge.

Luke calmly said to Skye, "The sticks are just next to your right hand. Grab them now."

Skye, whose eyes mirrored her terror, reached aggressively for our sticks. Both Addy and I had to steady ourselves against the strength of her grasp.

Luke, urgently said, "Leira, Addy, start backing up now!"

We began backing up slowly, praying the sticks wouldn't break, and that none of us would fall. Suddenly, I became aware of Luke's shuddering body, and I realized, he'd lost all his strength and his muscles were shaking from exhaustion. Panicked, I commanded Addy, "PULL! PULL HARD—NOW!"

With a burst of energy we didn't know we had, Addy and I watched in amazement as Skye slid up over the edge! We kept pulling until she was safely on solid ground. All three of us burst out in tears of happiness and exhaustion as Skye began crawling towards us. Then, remembering my concern for Luke, I glanced down towards him. He was lying lengthwise next to the drop-off. He wasn't moving, so I quickly made my way down to him, anxiously asking, "Luke, are you OK? Give me your hand so I can move you away from the ledge." Apparently, our pulling Skye from above and Luke gripping her other hand while we did so had shifted him into a dangerous position. When he didn't respond to my question, I noticed his chest rise and fall and thought to myself, "He's just exhausted." As I neared him, Skye called out, "Be careful Leira, the ground gives way!"

Frightened more than ever, I reached out for his limp hand. The instant I picked up his hand, the ground gave way beneath him. Everything seemed to happen in slow motion as I watched Luke slowly topple over the edge, and my hand, which had barely been able to grasp his, slipped away from Luke's. At that same instant, I realized I was losing my balance and would shortly follow Luke over the edge. As I was about to plummet downwards, I felt a dreadful and painful yank on my hair!

Shocked, I turned around and saw Skye and Addy hanging on to my hair. With tears streaming down my face, I whispered, "You can let go now, I'm safe." Then, I glanced towards the cliff edge and began sobbing.

Addy immediately yelled, "STOP IT! HE WILL BE FINE! Both of you pull yourselves together and let's CAREFULLY see where he is. He needs OUR help now. We don't even know what's happened to him. So, stop your stupid crying and see how to help him."

Skye, still crying, responded angrily, "Don't you understand? It's my entire fault! If I hadn't slipped, this never would have happened."

Then, Addy did something none of us expected; she slapped Skye across the face! Immediately following that, she stated, "Are you going to stand there feeling sorry for yourself or help Luke?"

A bright outline appeared on Skye's face where Addy had hit her. Skye rubbed her cheek and said quietly, "No one has ever slapped me and gotten away with it except my brother Liam."

Addy, feeling alarmed, was just about to apologize, when Skye said seriously, "Thanks Addy, you were right. Let's see how we can help Luke."

I was anticipating the worst had happened to him, so my friend's squabble was the last thing I was worried about. Addy, on the other hand, seemed to have turned into someone I didn't know. She told Skye to go up to the backpacks and get out the ropes Luke had used to hang the canvas sacks from the trees. Skye obeyed without complaint. Addy and I were surveying the area when Skye arrived back with the two ropes. Addy tied them to the strongest-looking tree. Turning, she looked at me and stated, "Leira, I'm going to tie this around your waist and you're going to lean over that edge and find Luke. Ready?"

I felt as if I was in a trance as I stood up and walked towards Addy. She tied a solid knot around me, and Skye double-checked it. Addy then lead me to the solid part of the edge, and both she and Skye gradually released the rope inch by inch until I was hanging out over the canyon. Still in a daze, I heard Addy ask, "Well, do you see him?" Skye irritably prodded, "WELL! Can you see him or not?"

Roughly coming back to my senses, I nervously said, "Not yet. Just don't let go of the rope!" Both Skye and Addy quickly replied, "We won't."

Terrified, not only by my precarious position, but also by what I might see below, I began scanning for Luke. I squinted my eyes as I tried to search the canyon floor about five hundred yards away. But, I couldn't find him. Suddenly, I felt a tiny spark of hope and yelled, "WAIT! I see something lying on a ledge, but I'm not sure what. Give me a couple more inches of rope."

Sensing they were nervous about my request, I called back to them, "What are you waiting for?" They rechecked their footing and knew they had a good hold on me, so they finally gave me another three or four inches of rope. It was then that I spotted him!

Approximately fifteen to twenty feet below me was a small rock ledge, surrounded by brush growing out of the side of the canyon wall. Luke was lying sideways on the ledge with both arms entangled in the brush. He wasn't moving, but maybe—just maybe—he had only gotten a bump on his head. I yelled to Skye and Addy to pull me back, which they carefully did. As I turned to face them, the looks on their faces were soul wrenching.

Hurriedly I explained, "I saw him. He's landed on a ledge with scrub brush that might have broken his fall, but he's not moving. Somehow, we have to get down there and help him."

Addy quickly spoke up, "What about the ropes? Couldn't we lower you down, Leira?"

I replied dejectedly, "No. They're too short."

Skye interjected, "Why don't Addy and I look through the packs and see if we can come up with something. You stay here in case he calls out."

I said, "OK, but try and be quick about it."

Addy and Skye moved out of sight while I sat down, trying to think of some other way to help Luke. Every now and again, I called out his name, but he didn't answer.

Addy and Skye returned about fifteen minutes later. Noticing they weren't carrying anything, I cried out in frustration, "YOU DIDN'T FIND ANYTHING THAT WILL HELP?"

Addy looked distressed as Skye said, "Leira, we looked through everything. Other than our dirty pants, which we could string together, or cutting all the straps off our packs, we couldn't find anything useful. We thought about the sleeping bags, but couldn't think of a way they would help, even if we zipped all four of them together."

I said to Addy, "Don't worry, we'll think of something. It's not going to help Luke if we don't keep calm."

Skye suggested, "Why don't I try and hike up to the jeep? We're about halfway back. I think I might be able to find it. It's possible the cell phone Luke left in the jeep would work from there."

I thought over what she said and replied, "That's a great idea Skye!" After we talked it over a few minutes, Addy said dismally, "I see two problems: one, you might get lost and two, Luke has the keys to the jeep in his pocket."

After hearing Addy's input, I said, "I don't think you should go. Besides, I don't want to take the chance that you might get lost or injured." Addy nodded her head, wiped her eyes and sniffled.

Skye hesitantly said, "We've got another problem, Leira."

Aggravated, I asked, "What else could possibly be wrong?"

Skye replied, "Addy and I don't have any water left in our canteens. We checked yours, and it's more than half-empty. Addy and I both talked it over and we're pretty sure the next spring is across the desert plateau at the top of this trail. What do you think?"

Quickly looking at my watch, then back at my friends, I said, "It's already one-thirty. How long do you think it would take to hike to the spring and are you absolutely sure you know where to go?"

Addy replied, "I'm positive! We'll leave a trail of stones, sticks or pebbles on the plateau. If we don't find the spring within thirty to forty minutes, we'll be able to get back no problem. What do you think Skye?"

Skye replied, "That'll work, no problem."

I contemplated a moment and then, finally agreeing said, "Alright, but if you two aren't back within two hours, then I'll have to come looking for you! While you're gone, I'll keep trying to get a response from Luke. Take his canteen to fill up, and I'll keep mine." I glimpsed back over toward the cliff and said worriedly, "He's going to need water when he's awake." Observing my friends, I said, "Hurry up. Take the last two sticks, and be sure to return by three-thirty. One more thing, grab Luke's emergency kit from his backpack—just in case."

Addy and Skye started hiking upwards around the curve. Once again, I called out to my cousin, "LUKE! CAN YOU HEAR ME? CAN ANYONE HEAR ME? PLEASE, WE NEED HELP!"

Chapter 16

Evening Nears

As I listened to the last traces of Skye and Addy's footsteps, I felt a deep sense of despair hovering over me. Not only was my cousin hurt—or worse, but also my two best friends were heading off into the desert full of wild animals, reptiles and insects, with only a slight idea of where they were going. I had never felt so helpless or afraid in my life. I kept calling to Luke every few minutes, hoping he would respond, but as the tears fell from my eyes, I couldn't help but imagine the worst.

———◦◦◦✦◦◦◦———

Meanwhile, Addy and Skye had successfully found the spring near the base of the steep hill. Feeling confident, they filled the canteens with water and headed back.

Skye exclaimed to Addy, "I knew we could find it! Now we just need to figure out what we can do to help Luke. At the very least, I now know where to start the hike up to the jeep and get some food. If we're really lucky, the cell phone will work from there."

Addy cheered up, but then reminded Skye about the keys. Addy continued, "We'll have to think about that part. Let's hurry back and discuss it with Leira."

Skye thought to herself, "Well, that all depends upon whether Luke is alive and if we can help him up, not to mention if the cell phone works." Gazing at the waning sunlight, she added to herself, "And we need to finish before night-time." Skye gave Addy a reassuring smile, but somehow it fell a little short.

Continuing their journey back, Skye kept gazing at her watch. Addy noticed and asked, "Are we late or something?"

Skye replied irritably, "Yeah, I told Leira we would be back by three-thirty!"

Addy questioned, "Well, what time is it?"

Skye responded tersely, "It's almost three-thirty!"

Addy questioned defensively, "Why are you angry at me?"

Skye started trotting, and replied, "I'm not mad. I'm upset because we only have another fifteen or twenty minutes to get back. If we don't hurry, Leira might come after us. Let's get moving!"

At that instant, Addy yelled, "Skye, WATCH OUT!" Before Skye knew what was happening, she ran straight into a prickly pear cactus—again!

She stumbled, falling awkwardly to the ground, and gasped out in agonizing pain. There were almost a hundred spines embedded in her right arm and leg!

Addy was beside her immediately, and with tears coursing down her face, she cried, "I'm so sorry! If I hadn't been distracting you, this never would have happened."

Skye snapped, "It was my own clumsiness. Find the ointment from Luke's emergency kit and help me get these spines out."

Addy, looking slightly overwhelmed, replied tearfully, "OK..."

Skye bravely withstood the pain by maintaining her focus on the greater problem—Luke.

After Addy and Skye pulled out the spines and patched her up as best as possible, they continued through the desert as quickly as they were able. They knew that because of the accident they would be back later than they should be. They were both hoping and praying that Luke and Leira were all right.

Back at the drop off, fear was starting to overwhelm me. My friends were gone, my cousin was unconscious or dead, and I had no idea what to do next. As three-thirty came and went, I started panicking, trying to decide what to do. Should I go off in search of my friends or remain with Luke in case I could help?

When four o'clock arrived, I knew I had to make some kind of decision. It would start getting dark in another two hours and I was sure I couldn't make it back to the jeep with the sunlight fading. I had run out of water, and Luke was still not responding.

Petrified, and overwhelmed by my emotions, I burst out sobbing.

A few moments later, my heart soared as I heard Skye's breathless but anxious voice, "What is it Leira? Did something happen? Is Luke OK?"

I looked up, and unbelievably, there was Skye, crouched down beside me. She searched my eyes in concern. Addy was next to her, waiting for my response.

Crying and laughing at the same time, I replied, "No, nothing's changed, except my best friends came back!" Then, noticing the filled canteens, I cried with relief, "And you've got water. You really found the spring."

Skye nodded smiling, and while handing me the canteen, she asked, "Has Luke made any sound or movement?"

I said, "No…but, I'm pretty sure he's alive. I've seen his chest move slightly. Hopefully, I'm not imagining it."

Looking down at my watch, I noticed it was twenty minutes after four o'clock, so I glanced at Skye and Addy and asked, "Why were you gone so long? Were you wrong about how long it took to reach the spring?"

Skye, looking a bit embarrassed, replied, "Well, it did take a little bit longer, because on the way back, I was hurrying so you wouldn't worry about us, and I ran into another cactus. Anyway, Addy came to the rescue and helped me pull out the spines and use the ointment from Luke's medicine kit."

Addy blushed at the compliment, but refused to take any credit for her behavior.

I said to both of them, "Luke would be proud of you—BOTH of you!" Thinking of him, the three of us looked down and shouted "LUKE!"

There was no response.

Glimpsing toward the lowering sun, I said, "We have to decide what to do. I've been thinking it over since you've been gone and one option is for one or two of us to hike up to the jeep with the flashlight and try to use the cell phone."

Addy chimed in, "That's exactly what Skye suggested on the way back!"

Nodding my head, with a smile, I said, "I'm glad we're all thinking the same way."

"Another idea I had was for the three of us to go to the jeep. I don't want to leave Luke alone, but when darkness falls, I'm not sure how any of us will react alone." I dropped my voice to a whisper at that statement to let each of them consider the situation.

Gazing at my friend's concerned and bleak faces, I added, "The only other thing I could think of was to try and unpack the tent, pick some cactus to eat while it's still light enough and hope someone comes looking for us. What do you think?"

I knew our options were slightly pitiful, but they were all I could think of at that time. As neither of them responded, I asked impatiently, "Well, do either of you have a better suggestion?"

Addy and Skye shook their heads no.

I said, "All right then. Addy, could you go gather some cactus?" Skye cringed at that question. "Skye, can you manage to get Luke's tent? The three of us should be able to figure out how to set it up. I'll wait here in case Luke wakes up. Are there any questions?"

Addy timidly asked, "What if I see a snake?"

With an empty stomach and fear surging through me, I angrily replied, "HISS AT IT!"

Alarmed at my uncharacteristic response, Addy immediately replied, "OK."

Upset by my awful outburst, I tried to offset my angry words, "Addy, I'm really sorry, I didn't mean to be nasty. I'm just afraid for Luke. Please forgive me."

Addy, always the most cheerful of us, replied, "That's alright Leira. I understand. I'm sorry I'm worrying more about myself, when it's Luke who's in trouble."

I said, "Thanks Addy, you're a good friend. I know the three of us are scared. But, if we put our heads together and remember everything Luke has taught us, I'm sure everything will turn out all right. Agreed?" I smiled, raised my eyebrow, cocked my head and waited for their response.

Both of them smiled slightly and nodded in agreement. Then, Skye left to fetch the tent and Addy went with her to get utensils and gather the cactus for our dinner. Meanwhile, I watched Luke and called to him every few minutes while they were away.

Skye returned first with the tent. She said, "I know he opened this within a minute, but I can't figure out how. Can you?"

Regretfully, I replied, "No, not really, but we should be able to figure it out, don't you think?"

Skye replied skeptically, "I can't. Not without instructions."

Pursing my lips, I said hopefully, "Well, Addy gets straight A's on her report card, so maybe she can figure it out. Last week she told us she could build anything."

Skye added a bit sarcastically, "She said that she could do that ONLY if she had instructions."

Regretfully, I replied, "Oh yeah, I forgot that part." Addy returned with the torn rain flysheet holding several pieces of cactus.

She hastily inquired, "Has there been any change?"

I replied, "No, nothing yet."

Skye said in exasperation, "We're doing nothing to help him! Can't the three of us come up with something?"

I looked at Skye, frustrated and replied angrily, "I haven't the foggiest idea how to help! I'm terrified! What do YOU think I should do—climb down there somehow?"

Addy quickly interjected, "NO! We don't need you dangling off the side of a cliff!"

Skye took a deep breath and said seriously, "Addy, give me my share of the cactus. After that, I'm heading for the jeep. It's the only way to help Luke. I know the way pretty well. I'm so angry with myself for not continuing on when we got to the spring. I would have been at the jeep by now and have already phoned for help."

I told Skye, "I'm sorry for my outburst." Then looking at her reassuringly, stated, "Skye, when you wanted to hike to the spring, none of us were thinking very clearly. Besides, you weren't even positive you could find the spring, but you did. At the spring, there's only one hike up to the jeep, but it'll be dark before then. I know how brave, stubborn and determined you are, but I'm scared for you…"

Addy contributed one last piece of advice, "Skye, even if you happen to make it, you don't have the keys to get into the jeep. They're in Luke's pocket—remember? I don't think you should go."

Skye replied sarcastically, "I don't need keys to get into that jeep, just a good piece of wood or stone! I may get stuck with a few cactus spines here or there but if I don't go then Luke might…." She couldn't bring herself to finish the statement, so she waited for our reply.

Addy prompted, "Might what?"

I elbowed Addy hard in the ribs.

Skye smiled and said, "Marry me of course!"

Laughing, at Skye's light-hearted reponse, I agreed, but I was terrified that I would lose my cousin and one of my best friends. Setting aside my selfish fears and trusting my best friend, I added, "Well, take the flashlight, emergency kit, a walking stick and a canteen. If, no—WHEN, you reach the jeep and get the cell phone, just dial 911." For some strange reason, I wanted to say, "May the force be with you." Instead, I said, "Be careful, use your stick and remember everything Luke has taught us." Then I gave her a big hug.

Addy's eyes filled with tears, but she murmured to Skye, "Watch out for those prickly pear cacti."

Skye looked at us with a glimmer of a smile and with her possessions in hand, started the long trek back to the jeep. It was about five o'clock and we all knew the sun would set before she reached her destination. Addy and I glanced at one another with fear and concern etched on our faces.

Chapter 17

Face to Face

As Skye disappeared from view, Addy and I quietly went about taking the spines off our 'dinner'. Addy remarked as she began eating, "This tasted much better when Luke made it for us—not to mention that I have stabbed myself a couple hundred times." I replied, "Well, at least we have something to eat because of what Luke taught us."

Inwardly, I kept my irritation with Addy to myself, as I thought of Luke, who hadn't had anything to eat or drink for several hours. After dwelling on Luke's thirst and hunger, suddenly, I came up with an idea.

"Addy!" I said urgently, "Luke needs water. Maybe we can find a way to lower a canteen down to him and give him a nudge with it. Skeptically, Addy looked at me and asked, "What good would that do?"

Frustrated, I answered, "We can leave the canteen slightly open and dribble water into his mouth."

Addy responded enthusiastically, "Leira, you're brilliant! Let's go check out what we have and find a rope or something we can do this with."

I followed Addy hastily up to our baggage and said cautiously, "Remember, keep an eye out for snakes or whatever."

Addy immediately halted in her tracks. Glancing back at me, she replied sarcastically, "Thanks for reminding me of that!" After a moment, she added with regret, "Sorry, I appreciate your warning. I mean it—I'm really sorry."

I replied, "No problem. Let's just get going and see if our plan helps Luke."

As we ruffled through our backpacks, we came across some unnoticed additional cording which Luke must have packed in case the ropes used to raise up the bags of food and garbage weren't enough. Looking at Addy with excitement, I said, "I'm pretty sure this will work."

Addy replied, "I just hope it's long enough. Let's go!"

———◦◦◦❖◦◦◦———

Meanwhile, as we were heading back to the site, Skye was trudging through the desert, keenly watching for cactus, insects, snakes—or worse, animals. By the time she reached the spring she had visited earlier, she was kicking herself for not having continued on the first time. Stoically, she filled her canteen and began the long hike up towards the jeep. The sun was fading more quickly than she anticipated, but with her walking stick, flashlight and canteen swinging from her side, she continued her exhausting climb.

———◦◦◦❖◦◦◦———

At that same moment, Addy and I attached the cord to Luke's canteen. Keeping my thoughts focused on the immediate task, I told Addy, "I'm going to leave the lid of the canteen slightly ajar. We have to be especially careful to keep the canteen from spilling little-or-any water. If we can wake Luke up, he'll be able to drink it. But, even if we can't wake him, maybe we'll be lucky enough to dribble some water into his mouth. Are you ready?"

111

Addy nodded in agreement. Slowly, we dropped the canteen downwards and eventually it reached Luke. We maneuvered the canteen together so it bumped him slightly several times. Unfortunately, there was no response. Looking over at Addy, I said, "I'm worried." With tears starting to stream down my face, Addy replied confidently, "He's going to be just fine! Now let's try to dribble some water in his mouth. Remember, Skye is on her way to get help, so everything will be all right."

Taking courage from Addy's positive attitude, I gathered my emotions together and said, "Sorry, Addy, let's try and lower this canteen into a better position, and trickle some water into his mouth."

We were holding the canteen with two separate cords, so we could manipulate it. Carefully, we moved it into a position above Luke's mouth, although it seemed to take a very long time. Neither of us looked away from our target, afraid we would mess up. With little water left, we didn't want to make any mistakes. Quietly, I whispered to Addy, "I'm going to raise my end up a tiny bit at a time. You just hold your end still and it should work. OK?"

Addy whispered, "All right—I'm steady—do it now."

Slowly, a fraction of an inch at a time, I lowered my cord, waiting to see if the position was correct. When I thought it was about right, I quietly said to Addy, "Don't move." She didn't, and as I lowered my end the slightest bit, I watched intensely with relief as water trickled over and into Luke's mouth.

Neither Addy nor I spoke a word or breathed (I think), as we kept the process up. During the nerve-wracking experience, we thought we heard Luke make a few feeble coughs. We stopped to make sure we weren't giving him too much at once. Finally, when we were sure we had gotten enough water into him for the time being, we co-coordinated the canteen's movement upwards, so as not let any more water trickle out. Neither of us wanted to hike back to the spring in the dark as the sun was setting.

After safely retrieving the canteen, we both felt slightly uplifted."

Addy said, "I think because of what we've just done that he'll be all right. My mom worked at a nursing home for a few years and I've heard some of her experiences about people who've died. Luke looks fine, and his coughing means he's all right for now. I think if Skye makes it to the jeep, then he'll be OK."

Trying hard to cover up my worries, I replied to Addy, "Thanks. Let's just hope Luke regains his consciousness soon, or that Skye is able to reach the jeep and cell phone quickly."

Addy said, "I totally agree. Skye should be near the jeep by now."

I added a bit fearfully, "I'm really worried about her. I hope she reaches it without any problems."

Addy acknowledged by nodding and then said, "Let's have a little more cactus before it gets too dark. Oh, and before we give Luke more water let's figure out how to open the tent."

We began figuring out how to set up the tent while dusk was creeping upon us. Addy—the brainy one among us figured it out within minutes. She told me, "I know how to open this, but it can't be done here. We'll have to bring it to the spot where we originally left our stuff. It's flatter there. Is that all right?"

I nodded and replied, "Well…we don't have any choice at this point. Looking down at Luke, I said over my shoulder to Addy, "Hurry—won't you? We'll need to give Luke some more water."

Confidently, Addy replied, "Don't worry, I'll be right back."

More than a mile away, Skye was beginning to ascend the last upward climb toward the jeep. She was nearly one-third of the way to the top when the roar of a mountain lion stopped her dead in her tracks!

Down in the canyon, Addy had successfully set up the tent. She thoroughly went through our sleeping bags (as Luke had shown us), prior to zipping the tent closed. Satisfied that she had covered everything, she headed back down to me, to report on her achievements. Shortly after arriving, she asked, "Do you have a plan now, Leira? Should we wait for Skye, or stay up all night keeping a watch on Luke?"

Irritably, I responded, "We can't leave Luke!"

Addy replied softly, "I'm sorry, Leira."

After a moment of consideration and regret, I said, "Addy, It's not you who should be sorry—it's me. You've been terrific, and so has Skye. I just feel so helpless. I don't know what else to do but pray that a miracle occurs, because there is no way we can climb down there, unless Skye gets to the jeep and can call for help….", At that, I began sobbing.

Addy abruptly interrupted me, stating severely, "LEIRA JEAN MACGREGOR! You listen to me now! Skye will be reaching the jeep any minute now, and we'll keep lowering more water to Luke. Then we'll take turns sleeping in the tent. So—for now, let's get busy giving Luke more water! Agreed?"

Looking up teary-eyed, I nodded my head and we spent the next half hour lowering the canteen to Luke and dribbling water into his mouth. I was almost positive I saw movements in his chest, and desperately hoped I wasn't imagining it.

Addy said afterwards, "I know you're exhausted, even if you won't admit it. Why don't you try and get some rest? I'll take the first shift for one hour. It's seven o'clock now. At eight o'clock, I'll switch places with you and nap for an hour. What do you think?"

I replied, "Well, you're right that I won't sleep, but maybe some time to rest and think about what else we can do to help, will do me some good." Tentatively, I asked Addy, "Are you positive you're OK with staying here alone?"

Addy answered without her usual hesitation, "I'm fine! Really!"

I began to climb the embankment to the tent. The sun had almost completely set. Just as I was about to unzip the tent, I looked up at the remnants of the pinkish sunset in the sky and in the forefront of the rocky hill in front of me, I spotted the outline of what I hoped were two people. But, their appearance seemed unusual. They were moving towards me at a steady pace. There was no doubt I would shortly come face to face with whoever—or—whatever had found us! Desperately, looking around for something to defend myself with, I succumbed to the oldest known ailment, caused by exhaustion and fear. I fainted.

Chapter 18

To the Rescue!

Groggily, I awoke to a fragrant aroma. Blinking my eyes several times in the twilight, I started to make out the features of an old wrinkled and careworn man, but his eyes were seemingly wise. His hair was very long and silvery in the waning light. Next to him was a young teenage boy. He had lengthy, shiny black hair with some sort of band around his deeply tanned forehead. The old man was speaking to me, but I couldn't understand a word he was saying. Shaking my head and blinking my eyes again, I whispered hoarsely, "What's happening? Who are you?" Slowly, I realized they were Native Americans and a sense of relief filled me. From all I had learned from Luke and even in school, I had nothing to fear.

The boy responded, "In your language, I am called Rob. This is my grandfather, 'Yellow Nose', who is Shaman of our tribe. I'll explain later. Your friend needs our help now. Let us go to him."

Suddenly, the whole terrible situation came rushing back to me! I sprang up quickly, wavered dizzily for a second, and then cried out in anguish, "LUKE! We need to help my cousin Luke!"

As I turned and began to hurry back towards Luke, I stumbled. Rob caught my arm and steadied me. He said, "Take hold of my hand, I will lead you. My grandfather had to use smoke from his medicine bag to revive you, and you're still affected by it."

"OK." I replied slowly. So many thoughts were going through head that I couldn't give any other response. Horrible images of Luke lying on the ledge were crossing my mind. Addy was waiting for me and I didn't know how long I had been gone. Skye was off somewhere in the darkening desert night trying to find her way to the jeep. Exhausted as I was, I looked at my watch, and pushed the button to light it up. I saw to my distress that it was after eight o'clock.

I managed to ask Rob, while continuing to stumble towards Luke, "Where's my flashlight? I can barely see."

Rob replied, "I have it. We do not need it just yet. What has happened to your cousin Luke?"

Softly, I replied, "He saved my best friend Skye from falling over the cliff, but the ground gave way because of the heavy rain, and he fell onto a bushy rock ledge about twenty feet down." Frantically, I added, "My friend Skye went off into the desert alone, trying to find her way back my cousin's jeep, which has a cell phone to call for help."

By the time I finished talking, we had reached the area where Luke had fallen. Addy was sitting near the ledge, rocking back and forth with apparent anxiousness. Startled by our appearance, she became overwhelmed when she realized there were Indians with me.

She gasped, pointed, and whispered in a straggled voice, "Indians."

I quickly said, reassuringly, "It's alright Addy; they've come to help us."

Rob grinned a little as he said, "We prefer to be known as 'Native Americans'."

Addy blushed profusely, but remained quiet.

Within minutes, Rob's grandfather surveyed the situation. He immediately began to speak to his grandson in their native language. I didn't have clue as to what he was saying, but Rob quickly responded to follow his instructions.

Urgently, I asked Rob, "What's going on? What is he saying? TELL ME, please..."

Rob quickly replied, "Do not worry, just watch. My grandfather is a Shaman and very wise."

I questioned, "What the heck is a Shaman?"

Rob replied briskly, "Not now."

I moved over toward Addy and hunched down next to her. I quietly explained what had occurred so far and ended by saying, "I think they're going to help Luke. Let's just sit still and watch. If they need us, they'll let us know. I don't know why, but I trust them."

Addy whispered in awe, "They're real Indians, aren't they?"

I nodded, "That's why I trust them. Rob says his grandfather is a 'Shaman'. Do you know what that is?"

Addy looked a bit astonished as she replied, "A Shaman is a very important member of the tribe. Not only is he considered a 'Wise Man', but he's also extremely experienced in medicine."

Impressed, I watched, but didn't believe it, as 'Grandfather' climbed down over the cliff and disappeared!

I stood up immediately, and impatiently asked Rob, "What is he doing? He could get hurt or worse!"

Rob's long black hair shimmered in the moonlight as he turned toward me. With piercing dark eyes, he silenced me immediately. Addy was quick to catch on and tugged at my shirt, pulling me down next to her. Quietly, she said, "Let them do their work."

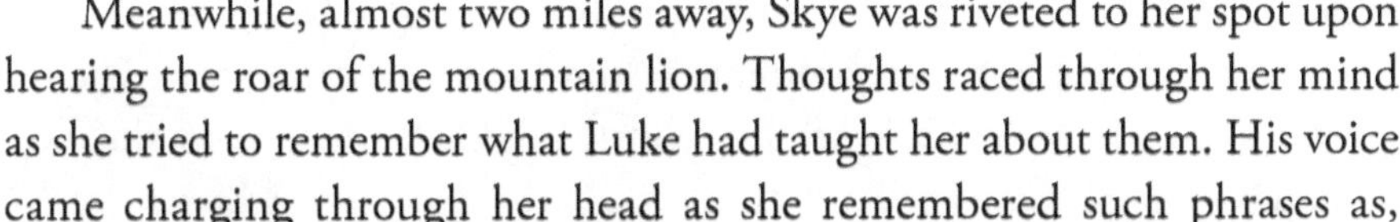

Meanwhile, almost two miles away, Skye was riveted to her spot upon hearing the roar of the mountain lion. Thoughts raced through her mind as she tried to remember what Luke had taught her about them. His voice came charging through her head as she remembered such phrases as, "Always avoid hiking alone, especially between dusk and dawn."

The sun disappeared from the horizon. Dusk had arrived and with it, Skye became understandably terrified. Grasping for something to hold on to, she recalled that Luke had also said, "If you are out at night, make a lot of noise, and always carry a walking stick. If you follow my advice, you shouldn't have any problems. Your scent and the noise will keep almost any animal away."

Skye held her walking stick tightly and began beating it loudly on her canteen. At the same time, she yelled, "I'M NOT AFRAID OF YOU! JUST TRY TO COME NEAR ME, AND I'LL GET YOU WITH MY STICK! YOU'RE NOTHING MORE THAN A BIG, BIG BULLY, JUST LIKE MY BROTHER, LIAM! HUH! SO THERE!"

Inside, Skye was shaking in her shoes, but with sheer determination, she continued her climb upwards to the jeep. She thought that if everything went well she would be there in a half hour—as long as the mountain lion didn't slow her down…

—◦◦◦)◦◦(◦◦◦—

Meanwhile, several more minutes passed as I quietly waited with Addy. Finally, my patience wore thin. I hesitantly approached Rob and asked, "What's he doing?"

Rob immediately replied, "Please be quiet. I am waiting for Grandfather's instructions."

At that moment, we heard the old Shaman speak to his grandson. Once again, we had absolutely no idea what was happening.

They spoke repeatedly to one another without Addy or I understanding a word and finally, I burst out pleading "IS HE ALIVE? Just tell me that!"

Rob spun around and gave me a quick nod before hurrying off up the trail and out of sight!

Anxiously, Addy asked me, "Where do you think he's going?"

I replied in anguish, "I have no idea. But I still believe they're here to help. So let's just try and focus on that, OK?"

Addy nodded, but then brought up another worrisome topic, "Leira, do you think Skye is all right? Do you think she's made it to the jeep by now?"

I replied, "I'm trying to be optimistic about that too. Let's hope she's there by now."

Addy nodded, and we both offered up a silent prayer for Luke and Skye.

—◦◦◦)◦◦(◦◦◦—

While we were worrying, Skye successfully eluded the mountain lion; at least she didn't hear it anymore. She continued to sing and occasionally bang her canteen even though she felt stupid. She figured that, at the very least, it would help keep animals away, and maybe someone would hear her and come investigate.

Her legs were aching painfully, but as she shone the flashlight upwards a bit through the darkness, her heart soared! Finally, she saw the end of the trail. In a few minutes, she would climb onto the plateau and arrive at the jeep with the cell phone waiting. Screaming out "YES", she hurriedly traipsed up the last several yards to the top. Suddenly, her elation abruptly stopped when she heard an extremely angry 'hissss'.

⸻ ∘∘❈∘∘ ⸻

As Skye was facing her new adversary, Addy and I waited impatiently for Rob's return. I had called down to his grandfather a few times. He responded once, but I didn't understand a word.

About twenty minutes later, when Rob arrived back, he was carrying two long 'poles' with Luke's sleeping bag apparently attached to them.

In total amazement, I looked at Rob and asked, "How did you do that, and WHAT are you going to do?"

Rob shook his head and replied, "No time for talk now. Help me lower this down to my grandfather now."

Instantly, Addy and I were by his side, listening intently to his instructions. He quickly showed us how he had fastened the bag to the poles with strong plant ties and partially using the ropes we had earlier, had lengthened them with more plant-made ropes. Then, he explained how we were going to lower it to the ledge where his grandfather would safely secure Luke.

His plan was impressive. I didn't dare question what they were doing. I simply trusted him and his grandfather. I felt Addy trusted them too, as in unison we lowered the 'makeshift' stretcher to the ledge.

We couldn't actually see what was happening, not only because of the slight overhang but it was completely dark now. I quietly asked Rob, "How can you see? You don't even have our flashlight lit. The only thing I can see are the stars, more stars than I've ever seen in my life..."

At that moment, a coyote began howling and then several joined in. My body (and Addy's) leapt a bit in fear.

Suppressing what I thought might be a chuckle; Rob said gently, "The coyotes are just 'singing'. There is nothing to be afraid of." Pausing a moment, he continued, "Grandfather sees 'everything'. He is a very wise man."

At that point, Rob's grandfather spoke to his grandson. After listening carefully, Rob turned to us and said, "Grandfather wants us to hold these ropes securely and slowly pull up your cousin. It is important that you listen to my instructions and make no move without them. Do you understand?"

I spoke out, "Yes. I understand." Addy nodded her head.

We watched as Rob tied two long ropes around the sturdiest tree, which produced a double set of ropes. Then, he dropped them down. He soundlessly walked over to Addy and I, then handed us the ends of the ropes. We silently waited as Rob wrapped the ropes around both our wrists and comfortably tugged them taut, but not painfully so.

Addy finally got up the nerve to ask, "And what are we supposed to do now?"

Rob replied, "Once Grandfather and I have everything set, I will tell you when to start backing up. I will be in between you to help. We will raise your cousin Luke up safely. Then Grandfather can finish his work."

Instantly, I asked, "What work?"

Hushing us, Rob replied, "Saving his life."

Chapter 19

Indian Medicine

Skye stopped dead in her tracks at the hissing sound. With her heart hammering in her chest, she cautiously looked around for the predator and prayed it wasn't the dreaded 'Western Diamondback Rattler'. Hearing another hiss as well as a rattle, Skye slowly shone her light towards the sound.

In total shock, Skye saw the diamond shapes along the snakes back and its pinkish color. Whizzing through her mind were memories—'Luke said the pink ones were beautiful—they demand the most respect—if I get bitten, I'm going to die—WHAT THE HECK AM I SUPPOSED TO DO?'

Digging deep into her soul for courage, she instinctively and slowly began to back up a few inches at a time. She tried to be as quiet as possible as she inch-by-inch backed away from the deadly snake. When she was a few feet away and out of striking distance, she began to talk quietly to the snake, sweeping her stick about a foot or two in front of it. Amazingly, the snake pulled back from its aggressive position, and slowly meandered away.

Skye—still too petrified to move, looked everywhere, listening intently for any hissing or roaring. Taking several deep breaths, she carefully resumed her final ascent to the jeep—AND—a cell phone. Gazing up at the stars, she whispered "Thanks."

As Skye was dealing with the snake, Addy, Rob and I began slowly pulling Luke up from the canyon ledge. He was very heavy, even with the three of us lifting him. As Rob's grandfather continued to direct from below, Rob explained exactly what to do. It took about seven or eight minutes to bring him up to our level. Then Rob stated, "I have to help Grandfather move him over the edge onto solid ground. Leira, you and Addy need to hold him stable until I can complete the task." Questionably, he asked, "Can hold him?"

Addy replied, "Let's do a quick test. Rob, stay where you are until we get in position, and then let go for a moment while we test the weight. If we can't hold him, you can grab back on."

Rob responded, "Good idea, pretty girl." Without pausing to notice the proud expression on Addy's face he said, "I'm letting go on the count of three. One-two-three!"

Addy and I were jerked slightly forward, but as we dug in our feet and leaned back, we steadied ourselves. We both felt confident that we could hold him. A moment later, we felt our load lighten and Rob asked, "Can you hold him?"

I replied quickly, "Yes. Go get him!"

Less than a minute later Addy and I watched in amazement how swiftly and assuredly, Rob moved and gently swung Luke back to the safety of solid ground. Addy and I hurried towards Luke's prone figure. Upon reaching him, we were completely astounded when Rob's grandfather appeared over the edge of the cliff!

Carefully, they moved Luke further away from the edge. Rob explained that his grandfather wanted to examine him on solid ground. After moving Luke about six feet from the ledge, they halted, and set him down. His grandfather began moving his hands swiftly but carefully over my cousin's body. At the same time, murmuring things to Rob.

Still frightened for Luke's life, I interrupted, "Will he be alright? What's your grandfather saying? Please, I need to know."

Rob replied, "Your cousin is alive and should recover, but he needs help. Grandfather says it's safe to carefully move him to where it is less treacherous, and where there is more moonlight."

His grandfather murmured another phrase and Rob translated, "He also says you have a good tent there to keep him in until help arrives."

Addy and I smiled in relief as Rob continued, "At the count of three, the four of us will lift and carry him to the tent. One, two, three!" With each of us holding a corner of the sleeping bag we had placed him on, we carefully lifted Luke and climbed up and around the embankment to the tent and the rest of our belongings. As we set him down, we watched in total amazement as Rob's grandfather poked and prodded. Finally, he closed his eyes while his palms hovered over every area of Luke's body. He seemed to be in a trance.

Rob kept a close eye on us, and intuition kept us silent. When his grandfather finally looked up, he spoke to Rob. Addy and I waited impatiently for his translation.

Eventually, Rob relayed to us, "My grandfather says that your cousin has several cracked ribs, a fractured leg and a concussion, which is why he has not been able to talk."

Noticing the fear and concern in our eyes, Rob continued, "Your cousin will be fine. Grandfather will bind his ribs, put a splint on his leg, and revive him afterwards with medicine he always carries. Tomorrow, after resting, when we are sure he is more comfortable, we will go for help. Do you have any questions?"

As Rob talked, his grandfather disappeared, and then returned with a flat piece of wood. He began to bind Luke's leg with some straps. We were too exhausted to ask where he had gotten them. Then, his grandfather set up fire to keep us warm against the night's oncoming chill.

Rob was still waiting for an answer, when I suddenly remembered Skye. I blurted out, "OH MY GOSH! Our best friend Skye was going to hike up to Luke's jeep and use his cell phone to call for help. She's out there in the dark all alone! Rob—could we go after her? Please..."

Rob relayed my request to his grandfather and while they spoke to each other, Addy and I couldn't understand a word they were saying. Shortly, Rob's grandfather handed him some items from his medicine bag and swiftly took off in the direction that Skye had gone.

Looking at Rob, we pleaded with our eyes for an explanation. Rob responded, "Grandfather said I could watch over your cousin. He gave me this medicine to help revive him, but also to relieve his pain. He said he would go after your friend. Grandfather is much more knowledgeable with the surroundings than I am and can travel faster."

Addy interrupted, "But he's so old. How can he move quicker than you?" As soon as she realized what she had said, Addy's face reddened in embarrassment.

Rob laughed a little and replied, "He may be old, but he is very agile, and much wiser in the desert than I am."

Addy, still blushing, replied, "I'm sorry. I didn't mean to insult your grandfather."

Rob grinned back and said, "No worries mate! By the way, you're doing well for being a 'Sheila' and all."

Addy and I were both astounded by his response, so I asked, "Hey! How can you possibly know the way Australians talk?"

Rob laughed and said, "Just because Grandfather and I came out here to explore our history, does not mean I do not have a television and DVD player at home."

"WHAT?" I exclaimed.

Rob laughed again and told us, "I do live on a reservation, but it is a great home. Grandfather is Shaman of our tribe and he has chosen me to carry on the tradition. He continuously brings me on retreats to learn the ways of our ancestors. I take it very seriously, even though I do like to watch movies!"

Cautiously, I asked, "What Indian tribe are you from?"

Rob answered, "We are Western Apache, although there are many different Apache tribes throughout the southwest. My family is also partly Chiricahua Apache, but together, all of the Apache tribes number only about five thousand now." At that statement, I noticed a distinct sadness in Rob's eyes, which were illuminated by the campfire.

Looking down at Luke's chest moving slowly up and down, I thought to myself, "I'm so lucky that Rob and his grandfather are here helping us today." I tried to remember what I had learned about Native American history from school but I couldn't remember much. If fact, I learned more about their way of life and their history in the last few days, than I had in any schoolbook. I suddenly understood that to fully understand something, you had to experience it—in one way or another.

When I looked at Rob, he surprised me by smiling. He nodded as if he had heard my thoughts. Then, we heard a slight, raspy, cough, and immediately turned towards Luke. He let out another tiny gasp and blinked his eyes, groaning in pain. Rob grinned and said to Addy and I, "He is going to be fine. Let me pour some of Grandfather's medicine down his throat to ease his pain. He is out of trouble now from the concussion and just needs time to heal."

I ran my hand over Luke's forehead, as Rob trickled the medicine down his throat. Then, my thoughts reverted to Skye. I wondered whether she had reached the jeep or if she was in trouble. I desperately hoped that Rob's grandfather would find her before anything went wrong.

Trying to wait patiently, I dribbled water into Luke's mouth. His moaning decreased as the medicine began to work. Rob listened to his breathing and said, "He is asleep now, so we will let him rest. Are either of you hungry?"

At that instant, both our stomachs growled loudly, and we nodded yes. Rob produced a bag of pemmican and a canteen from a pouch slung over his shoulder. He handed the bag and canteen to us.

Addy and I hastily grabbed pieces of pemmican and started chewing hurriedly. With her mouth still full of food, Addy managed to mumble out, "We have water."

As she reached for her canteen, Rob stopped her and held out his canteen to her. He said, "This has a very beneficial juice added to the water that will help strengthen you and calm your spirits. Please drink this instead."

I looked at him, and tentatively asked, "Is there anything illegal in here, like alcohol or...?" I couldn't continue because I was too embarrassed.

But Rob understood. Trying to suppress a laugh that was bubbling up inside him, he responded, "No, there is nothing like that in it. Just drink a bit and you will feel much better."

Meanwhile, Skye was elated as she reached the top of the climb and headed jubilantly toward the jeep. She sat down on a near-by rock to catch her breath and figure out how to bash in the window and get the cell phone. She got up and searched carefully for something strong enough to strike it with. Shining her light around, looking for a stout stick or large rock, her light pierced the blackness of the night, unveiling a bear, so close; she could see the breath exhaling from its nostrils! The only thing that crossed her mind was, "It's the same one we saw at the cliffs.", and with that, she crumpled to the ground, with the bear not fifteen feet away. She was unaware of the howl of the coyotes that were creeping towards her and the bear was closing in too!

Chapter 20

The Journey Back

As the coyotes neared, they picked up the scent of the bear and immediately disappeared into the night. The bear, seeing a human figure standing above him at the top of the precipice, stopped advancing.

Rob's grandfather began an old Indian chant praising the bear for once again warding off predators, while guarding and protecting the Apache and their friends. After several intonations of the chant, the bear lumbered off.

Nimbly, Rob's grandfather approached Skye. Touching her arm and head lightly, he realized she had fainted. He quickly produced from his medicine bag a small pouch from which he retrieved dried leaves, which he set alight. Slowly, he moved the drifting smoke near Skye's face. As the aroma and medicine-like qualities wafted into her nostrils, Skye groggily came to. She felt as if she was awakening from a dream. She hazily saw a human figure, kneeling before her, silhouetted by the moon. She asked, "Luke, is that you?"

Shortly thereafter, when her vision cleared, she perceived a very old man, and with her heart skipping a beat, she scurried backwards, letting out a shrill scream. It was a real American Indian!

Backing away, the old man said in a distinctly calming voice, "Skye, I am here to help you." He raised his arms in a type of peace offering. Skye was immediately heartened that he knew her name. Leira and Addy would have been astounded to learn that Rob's grandfather had understand everything they said, but for the moment, it was a secret between, Skye, Rob and his grandfather.

Rob's grandfather continued slowly, "I have come to help you, as my grandson and I have already helped Luke. He will be all right. Your friends, Leira and Addy have told me of your journey. Do not be afraid." He slowly swung his arms out in a circular motion that calmed Skye even more.

"If you will trust me, you can help your friends."

Glancing from side to side Skye questioned, "What about the coyotes and the bear I saw?"

She was surprised when the old man replied; "The bear is a friend of our tribe. He came to you when it was necessary, to ward off the coyotes. He has left now, but will return if needed. You have no cause to worry."

Skye, having trouble absorbing everything, said the first thing that came to her mind, "I need to break the window of the jeep to get Luke's cell phone and call for help. Can any of your Indian magic do that?"

Rob's grandfather shook his head. Noticing Skye's disappointment, he reached into his medicine bag and took out the keys he had taken from Luke's pants. Showing Skye the keys, he asked, "Will these help?"

Skye, laughed softly and said, "I hope so!" Rising to her feet with the help of Rob's grandfather, Skye thanked him. After opening the jeep door, she retrieved the cell phone. Then, she turned, looked at 'her new friend', and asked, "What is your name?"

The old man grinned and replied, "Yellow Nose or in Apache, 'Peet-saug – Bi-chee', but it is spelled much differently than it sounds."

Skye looked at him, completely bewildered, and asked, "I'm not even going to try to pronounce that. So what should I call you?"

Yellow Nose replied quietly, "Call me 'Grandfather'."

Skye nodded, and then turned her attention to Luke's cell phone. She couldn't figure out how to find Leira's, Aunt Debbie's number. After a minute or so, Rob's grandfather asked, "May I try?"

Skye gladly handed over the phone. Within a minute, Grandfather had dialed the number and handed it back to Skye.

When Leira's Uncle Ray answered the phone, he sounded very anxious. Skye told him what she knew and where she thought everyone was. Grandfather interrupted her to correct the location.

She handed the phone to 'Grandfather' and he relayed that they would be waiting to guide police and medical personnel to Luke.

Uncle Ray said he would immediately call for emergency assistance in the Sedona area.

Skye and Grandfather sat by the jeep and talked about what had happened. Less than a half-hour passed when they heard the sound of rugged vehicles nearing their area. Grandfather had just finished explaining to Skye that he only spoke Apache language unless it was necessary, as he wanted to keep the old ways and tongue alive amongst the tribe's people.

The local police and Reservation 'rescue' vehicles pulled alongside them. As they were questioned individually, Skye and Grandfather related what the situation was for their friends. Skye was speaking English to the local officers, while Grandfather simultaneously spoke in Apache to the Reservation police.

The conversation would have sounded like a bunch of babble to a passerby, but thankfully, everyone understood. The rescue squad was in contact with the medics, and told Skye and Grandfather they were on their way and should be there within minutes. The Police decided that one Sedona officer and one Reservation rescue officer would wait for the medic team to arrive while the other two trekked down to Luke. Grandfather would stay and guide the medics. One of the reservation police thought Skye might be hungry and thirsty, so he handed her a bag of pemmican, an apple, and a cool bottle of spring water.

As the two officers descended into the canyon, Skye called out while chewing a mouthful of pemmican, "Are you sure you know where you're going?"

Hesitating, the Sedona officer glanced awkwardly at the Native American officer for assurance. The Apache rescue officer grinned and gave Skye a 'thumbs up'.

Before Skye could finish her delicacy (as that's what it tasted like), she and the others heard the roar of the medic van climbing the rough hill. As soon as it arrived, about ten minutes later, Grandfather, the second Reservation rescue officer, and two medics left, carrying a portable stretcher and other medical gear.

Before following the rescue team, Grandfather said to Skye, "Summer Skye, you wait here with this officer and give thanks to the spirit above while we go see to your friend."

Skye replied, "Huh? What did you call me?"

Grandfather replied, "I name you 'Summer Skye' because to me, you are like a summer evening with a fragrant breath of wind. So stay, breathe in the fresh air and wait for us to return with Luke."

After the team had left, Skye looked up at the Sedona officer left behind and asked, "Will they be all right?"

The young officer reassuringly replied, "Your friends are in good hands. Why don't we call your parents and let them know help is on the way."

Skye grimaced, then, burst out, "MY PARENTS ARE IN CONNECTICUT! Do you want to call them there?"

The officer was slightly dumfounded and replied, "No, I'm sorry. I didn't know. We'll just wait for them to return. Then he added lamely, you could have more to eat if you'd like."

Skye looked at him dejectedly, and replied, "No thanks. I'll just keep watching for my friends—or coyotes—or BEARS!"

The officer peered around nervously. After a few moments he said, "Well, this might be a bit of a wait. I am going to sit in the rover. You can come with me and rest, if you want to until they get back. It might help pass the time."

Skye didn't answer immediately, so he nervously settled himself into the jeep. Unknown to Skye, he was new to the area and uncomfortable with 'desert creatures'. Before he closed the door, Skye replied, "No thanks, I'll wait out here for my friends, but if a scorpion or Tarantula appear, I might take you up on your offer." Skye had only one thought on her mind: would her friends appear over the edge with their rescuers, or not?

—∞◦◦—◦◦∞—

Meanwhile, Rob, Addy and I were getting anxious. The time passed slowly as we waited for help to arrive.

Shortly after Grandfather had left, I asked Rob, "How did you find us?"

Addy quickly tacked on, "Did YOU leave the signs, symbols—or whatever you call them—around our campsite?"

Rob grinned, and was about to reply when Luke gave an unusually labored sigh. The three of us turned toward him, Rob put his ear to Luke's chest and listened to his heartbeat as he checked his pulse simultaneously. Reassuringly, he said, "It is all right. He is just resting."

Addy and I heaved sighs of relief.

Evading our questions, Rob asked us, "The day you were almost upon the cliff dwellings, after you saw the bear, did you see a light within the caverns before you hurried away?"

Astonished, I answered, "YES! Skye and I both saw the light, but she didn't want to admit it!"

Addy asked irritably, "What are you talking about? I didn't see any light, and you NEVER said a thing about it to me!"

I tried to soothe Addy, "We were hurrying back and that was the night of the strange monsoon thunderstorm, or whatever it's called. I didn't even think about it until now. Be quiet and let Rob continue."

Addy reluctantly nodded her head, giving Rob permission to proceed.

He continued, "The light you saw was a fire Grandfather and I had burning to cook our evening meal." As Addy and I were about to interrupt, Rob signaled for us to let him finish.

He continued, "Grandfather is Shaman of our tribe. He has chosen me to follow in his footsteps. So, four times a year, ever since I was a small boy, he brings me to this land of our ancient ancestors and teaches me the old ways. He shows me how the Sinagua lived within the caves, how they climbed them, and how to evade hostile predators or tribes. By the way, it was much easier to creep through the tiny caverns when I was small! Your cousin might have told you how our ancestors were much smaller

131

than we are today." Grinning to himself, remembering earlier times, Rob closed his eyes. Opening them a moment later, he continued, "Grandfather and I had been in the desert for three nights. As we retraced areas visited previously, he explained more about our ancient culture, and what was happening now. He especially wanted me to understand the spirits—or, animals of the region. He also spoke about those who would do harm to our environment."

At that point, Rob's head hung a trifle, and I quietly asked, "You mean us? People who don't live here?"

Rob blushed and replied, "Not quite. Your cousin Luke is very sensitive to the surroundings and has shown you a good path."

The three of us looked at Luke, as Rob stated, "He has been very well trained in desert custom. I will tell him that when he awakens."

Turning her eyes away from Luke, Addy asked, "What about the symbols?"

Rob shook his head as if clearing it, and replied, "I'm sorry if they disturbed you. Grandfather was teaching me each night how to make symbols with rocks, sticks and writings to do several things. It was the first time he taught me the inscriptions. They included messages to help people, and ward off evil."

I looked at him in astonishment. Anger boiled up inside me, and I barked out, "What do you mean—ward off evil? My cousin is lying here in front of me and might die! My best friend almost died falling off a cliff, and now she's somewhere in the desert and hasn't returned for hours. To top it all off, we don't have any water left, and it's getting late!" As tears of exhausted frustration ran down my face, I felt two hands on my shoulders. Looking up, one was Addy's and the other belonged to Luke. Before lapsing back into unconsciousness, he murmured to me, "Don't worry Leira, everything will be fine."

Moments later, we heard the footsteps and voices of the medics and officers who had come to rescue Luke. In my heart, I knew he had already been rescued.

Rob saw his Grandfather and hurried over to speak with him. Returning, he assured us Skye was safe and that she and another officer were waiting for us at the jeep. I breathed a sigh of relief. The medics checked Luke thoroughly. They said he had two or three cracked ribs, a concussion and several sprains and bruises. Then they assured us he would be fine after they got him to a hospital.

I thought to myself, "He just needs a little loving care. And I bet Skye would like nothing more than to help."

The medics transferred Luke from the sleeping bag to a stretcher and began the hike back to the vehicles. Addy, Rob and I picked up what remained of our camping gear. After making sure we didn't leave anything behind, we caught up to the others.

Grandfather was in the lead, as we headed to the vehicles. Taking sips of water from the rescue squad bottles, Addy and I felt like life was pouring down our throats. It seemed like an incredibly long hike back, but we actually made good time.

We were surprised when we reached Luke's jeep to find another vehicle waiting. It was Uncle Ray's van. Apparently, he had just arrived. I was so relieved as I listened to his conversation with the medics, who assured him that Luke was going to be just fine.

I raced up to Uncle Ray to give him a hug, but in his traditional – 'Everything's great and it's no big deal attitude', I still thought I saw a tear in his eye—although I would never tell.

A few minutes later, Luke was on his way to Sedona Hospital.

Uncle Ray then called home. It was obvious to me that Aunt Debbie had answered the phone. I heard Uncle Ray telling her, "Hey! Everything's great here! The kids just got into the whole 'Indian' thing and were running late, so I've decided Luke isn't up to driving home tonight. So we're all going to hang out here for the night in Sedona and come home tomorrow!" Uncle Ray chuckled after that. I imagined Aunt Debbie wasn't too happy. But, I also believed when she heard the whole story she wouldn't be angry. I was sure she'd be thankful.

Prior to leaving, Addy, Skye and I approached Grandfather and Rob. I said to Rob, "We can't thank you and Grandfather enough for what you did. Luke could have died, or maybe even all of us. How can we repay you for your kindness and help?"

Then, looking at Rob, I asked, "I want to thank your Grandfather, but I don't know any Apache—can you translate for me?"

Skye looked at me as if I was stupid and asked, "Leira, what on earth are you talking about? He can speak English as well—or better than we can."

I looked at Skye and replied, "No he can't! Rob translates everything he says." I was interrupted as Rob cleared his throat a few times. Glancing at him, I saw he was trying not to laugh.

I asked in a perturbed voice, "What's so funny?"

Grandfather replied softly, "Leira, 'Little Butterfly', I can speak your language, but only if there is need."

I wanted to shout out, but somehow I knew I shouldn't. Grandfather continued, "When my grandson was able to translate, there was no need, but when I came upon your friend Skye, 'Summer Sky', as I will remember her by, I had no choice but to speak the language she would understand. That is all."

Lowering my head in understanding, I said the only thing left in my mind, "Thank you Grandfather."

He politely nodded his head and replied, "I am sure we will see each other again, Little Butterfly."

Addy asked one last question, "Grandfather, if Skye is 'Summer Sky' and Leira is 'Little Butterfly', what is my name?"

Grandfather replied, "Of course, your name will be remembered by my people as 'gah's isdzan'. Hearing his grandfather's reply, Rob blushed deeply and Addy asked, "What does that mean?"

Noticing Rob's reddening face, I asked him, "Could you tell us what that means?"

Rob shuffled his foot and while searching for an answer, and replied, "It means 'Rabbit's Woman'."

With our eyes darting amongst one another, we heard Uncle Ray shouting that we had to get going. Although we had more questions, they went unanswered. We shook hands with Rob and Grandfather. Before leaving, Rob whispered to Addy, "We'll see each other again."

Addy blushed, as the three of us hurried to the jeep. Piling into the vehicle, we could hear Grandfather's laughter as we heard him say to Rob, "Let's get going, Little Rabbit." Stunned, Addy, Skye and I suddenly realized why 'Grandfather' had named Addy 'Rabbit's Woman'! Rob liked Addy! I said, "Oh brother, another long distance relationship."

We arrived at a beautiful little B&B near the hospital. After devouring some food that Uncle Ray picked up on the way, Skye, Addy and I quickly fell asleep into a deep slumber.

The following morning we visited Luke and found out that he was going to be just fine, even though he was in quite a bit of pain. He said his head felt like a volcano had erupted. Surprisingly, he was in good spirits. Unfortunately, he wasn't going to be able to come home until the following day, which was when we were leaving. As we said our goodbyes, we were all a little teary-eyed. As I gave him a kiss on the forehead, I could see Skye would like to do the same.

Luke looked at each one of us and asked, "Didn't you have a good time?"

The three of us burst out laughing (and crying) and I replied, "We had a terrific time! But, the next time I come to visit, maybe we could just set up the tent in the backyard."

Luke replied grinning, while reminding us, "There are still coyotes, tarantulas, scorpions, wind spiders, black widows and several lizards that you might have to deal with, even in our back yard. But if you're up to it, I'll set aside the time!"

Addy and Skye looked concerned as I replied casually, "Well, maybe a good cookout will do, but….only if you make some prickly pear cactus with that awesome sauce."

Luke said, "You got it Butterfly! I hope all three of you can come back next year. Leira's got my e-mail address, so we can stay in touch." He gazed at each of us. I noticed Skye blush as Luke's eyes met hers.

Skye said, "Thanks for saving my life."

Luke replied, "Thanks for saving mine."

A nurse came into the room and prodded us to leave. With one last glance, we left his room. Skye had tears streaming down her cheeks. I gave her a hug, and said, "Don't worry; maybe you can come back next year! Besides, you've got e-mail."

We thoroughly enjoyed a comfy night at Aunt Debbie's, although it was a bit crowded. We woke early the next morning, packed, and got ready to go. Uncle Ray and Aunt Debbie drove us to the airport and we said our goodbyes. Taking our seats on the plane, Addy said, "Well, that was an adventure I'll never forget! I'm sure we'll look back on it someday and love telling the story, but right now I can't wait to get home and see my family and Katie-dog!"

Skye agreed and added, "I bet Shuger is really missing me, too!"

Addy and Skye were looking at me expectantly to say how much Fluffums must have missed me, but instead I replied, "Yeah, I can't wait to see Fluffums! But, I hope we can have another mystery or adventure, too!"

Leaning over to my mom, I asked, "Are you planning any more trips?"

My mom replied, "Eventually."

I asked quickly and quietly, "Can Skye and Addy come with us?"

Mom hesitated, and then finally said, "Let's just get everyone home safe and sound for now."

I sighed as I replied, "OK…" Little did I know that another mysterious adventure was creeping up on us back at home!